THE
PENDERWICKS

Awards for the Penderwicks series

Winner of the National Book Award for Young People's Literature

A Junior Library Guild Selection

A New York Public Library 100 Titles for
Reading and Sharing Selection

A *Child* Magazine Best Book of the Year

A *Kirkus Reviews* Best Book

A *Publishers Weekly* Best Children's Book

A *Publishers Weekly* Best Book of the Year

A *Booklist* Editors' Choice

A *School Library Journal* Best Book of the Year

A Book Sense Children's Summer Pick

A Texas Bluebonnet Award Master List Title

A Bank Street Best Book of the Year

Winner of a New England Book Award for Children's Literature

A Children's Indie Next Pick

THE
PENDERWICKS

A SUMMER TALE OF FOUR SISTERS,
TWO RABBITS,
AND A VERY INTERESTING BOY

JEANNE BIRDSALL

A YEARLING BOOK

For Bluey

Text copyright © 2005 by Jeanne Birdsall
Cover art and interior illustrations copyright © 2005 by David Frankland

All rights reserved. Published in the United States by Yearling, an imprint of Random House Children's Books, a division of Penguin Random House LLC, New York. Originally published in hardcover in the United States by Alfred A. Knopf, an imprint of Random House Children's Books, New York, in 2005.

Yearling and the jumping horse design are registered trademarks of Penguin Random House LLC.

Visit us on the Web! randomhousekids.com

Educators and librarians, for a variety of teaching tools, visit us at RHTeachersLibrarians.com

The Library of Congress has cataloged the hardcover edition of this work as follows:
Birdsall, Jeanne.
The Penderwicks : a summer tale of four sisters, two rabbits, and a very interesting boy / Jeanne Birdsall. — 1st ed.
p. cm.
Summary: While vacationing with their widowed father in the Berkshire Mountains, four young sisters, ages four through twelve, share adventures with a local boy, much to the dismay of his snobbish mother.
ISBN 978-0-375-83143-0 (trade) — ISBN 978-0-375-93143-7 (lib. bdg.) — ISBN 978-0-307-54134-5 (ebook)
[1. Sisters—Fiction. 2. Single-parent families—Fiction. 3. Vacations—Fiction. 4. Friendship—Fiction.] I. Title.
PZ7.B511P7Pe 2005 [Fic]—dc22 2004020364

ISBN 978-0-440-42047-7 (pbk.)

Printed in the United States of America
43

CONTENTS

THE
PENDERWICKS

CHAPTER ONE
A Boy at the Window

FOR A LONG TIME AFTER THAT SUMMER, the four Penderwick sisters still talked of Arundel. Fate drove us there, Jane would say. No, it was the greedy landlord who sold our vacation house on Cape Cod, someone else would say, probably Skye.

Who knew which was right? But it was true that the beach house they usually rented had been sold at the last minute, and the Penderwicks were suddenly without summer plans. Mr. Penderwick called everywhere, but Cape Cod was booked solid, and his daughters were starting to think they would be spending their whole vacation at home in Cameron, Massachusetts. Not that they didn't love Cameron, but what is summer without a trip to somewhere special? Then, out of the blue, Mr. Penderwick heard through a friend

1

of a friend about a cottage in the Berkshire Mountains. It had plenty of bedrooms and a big fenced-in pen for a dog—perfect for big, black, clumsy, lovable Hound Penderwick—and it was available to be rented for three weeks in August. Mr. Penderwick snatched it up, sight unseen.

He didn't know what he was getting us into, Batty would say. Rosalind always said, It's too bad Mommy never saw Arundel—she would have loved the gardens. And Jane would say, There are much better gardens in heaven. And Mommy will never have to bump into Mrs. Tifton in heaven, Skye added to make her sisters laugh. And laugh they would, and the talk would move on to other things, until the next time someone remembered Arundel.

But all that is in the future. When our story begins, Batty is still only four years old. Rosalind is twelve, Skye eleven, and Jane ten. They're in their car with Mr. Penderwick and Hound. The family is on the way to Arundel and, unfortunately, they're lost.

"It's Batty's fault," said Skye.

"It is not," said Batty.

"Of course it is," said Skye. "We wouldn't be lost if Hound hadn't eaten the map, and Hound wouldn't have eaten the map if you hadn't hidden your sandwich in it."

"Maybe it's fate that Hound ate the map. Maybe we'll discover something wonderful while we're lost," said Jane.

"We'll discover that when I'm in the backseat for too long with my younger sisters, I go insane and murder them," said Skye.

"Steady, troops," said Mr. Penderwick. "Rosalind, how about a game?"

"Let's do I Went to the Zoo and I Saw," said Rosalind. "I went to the zoo and I saw an anteater. Jane?"

"I went to the zoo and I saw an anteater and a buffalo," said Jane.

Batty was between Jane and Skye, so it was her turn next. "I went to the zoo and I saw an anteater, a buffalo, and a cangaroo."

"*Kangaroo* starts with a *k*, not a *c*," said Skye.

"It does not. It starts with a *c*, like *cat*," said Batty.

"Just take your turn, Skye," said Rosalind.

"There's no point in playing if we don't do it right."

Rosalind, who was sitting in the front seat with Mr. Penderwick, turned around and gave Skye her oldest-sister glare. It wouldn't do much, Rosalind knew. After all, Skye was only one year younger than she was. But it might quiet her long enough for Rosalind to concentrate on where they were going. They really were badly lost. This trip should have taken an hour and a half, and already they'd been on the road for three.

Rosalind looked over at her father in the driver's seat. His glasses were slipping down his nose and he was humming his favorite Beethoven symphony, the one about spring. Rosalind knew this meant he was thinking about plants—he was a professor of botany—instead of about his driving.

"Daddy," she said, "what do you remember about the map?"

"We're supposed to go past a little town called Framley, then make a few turns and look for number eleven Stafford Street."

"Didn't we see Framley a while ago? And look," she said, pointing out the window. "We've been past those cows before."

"Good eyes, Rosy," he said. "But weren't we going in the other direction last time? Maybe this way will do the trick."

"No, because all we saw along here were more cow fields, remember?"

"Oh, yes." Mr. Penderwick stopped the car, turned it around, and went back the other way.

"We need to find someone who can give us directions," said Rosalind.

"We need to find a helicopter that can airlift us out of here," said Skye. "And keep your stupid wings to yourself!" She was talking to Batty, who, as always, was wearing her beloved orange-and-black butterfly wings.

"They're not stupid," said Batty.

4

"Woof," said Hound from his place among the boxes and suitcases in the very back of the car. He took Batty's side in every discussion.

"Lost and weary, the brave explorers and their faithful beast argued among themselves. Only Sabrina Starr remained calm," said Jane. Sabrina Starr was the heroine of books that Jane wrote. She rescued things. In the first book, it was a cricket. Then came *Sabrina Starr Rescues a Baby Sparrow, Sabrina Starr Rescues a Turtle*, and, most recently, *Sabrina Starr Rescues a Groundhog*. Rosalind knew that Jane was looking for ideas on what Sabrina should rescue next. Skye had suggested a man-eating crocodile, who would devour the heroine and put an end to the series, but the rest of the family had shouted her down. They enjoyed Jane's books.

There was a loud *oomph* in the backseat. Rosalind glanced around to make sure violence hadn't broken out, but it was only Batty struggling with her car seat—she was trying to twist herself backward to see Hound. Jane was jotting in her favorite blue notebook. So they were both all right. But Skye was blowing out her cheeks and imitating a fish, which meant she was even more bored than Rosalind had feared. They'd better find this cottage soon.

Then Rosalind spotted the truck pulled over by the side of the road. "Stop, Daddy! Maybe we can get directions."

Mr. Penderwick pulled over and Rosalind got out of the car. She now saw that the truck had TOMATOES painted in large letters on each of its doors. Next to the truck was a wooden table piled high with fat red tomatoes and, behind the table, an old man wearing worn blue jeans and a green shirt with HARRY'S TOMATOES embroidered across the pocket.

"Tomatoes?" he asked.

"Ask if they're magic tomatoes," Rosalind heard. Out of the corner of her eye, she saw Skye hauling Jane back in through the car window.

"My younger sisters," said Rosalind apologetically to the old man.

"Had six of 'em myself."

Rosalind tried to imagine having six younger sisters, but she kept coming up with each of her sisters turned into twins. She shuddered and said, "Your tomatoes look delicious, but what I really need is directions. We're looking for number eleven Stafford Street."

"Arundel?"

"I don't know about any Arundel. We're supposed to be renting a cottage at that address."

"That's Arundel, Mrs. Tifton's place. Beautiful woman. Snooty as all get-out, too."

"Oh, dear."

"You'll be fine. There are a couple of nice surprises over there. You're going to have to keep that blond

6

one under control, though," he said, nodding toward the car, where Skye and Jane were now leaning out of the window together, listening. Muffled complaints could be heard from Batty, who was being squashed.

"Why me?" called Skye.

The man winked at Rosalind. "I can always spot the troublemakers. I was one myself. Now, tell your dad to go down this road a little ways, take the first left, then a quick right, and look for number eleven."

"Thank you," said Rosalind, and turned to go.

"Hold on a minute." He plopped a half-dozen tomatoes into a paper bag. "Take these."

"Oh, I can't," said Rosalind.

"Sure you can. Tell your dad they're a present from Harry." He handed Rosalind the bag. "And one last thing, young lady. You and your sisters better stay clear of Mrs. Tifton's gardens. She's touchy about those gardens. Enjoy the tomatoes!"

Rosalind got back into the car with her bag of tomatoes. "Did you hear him?"

"Straight, then left, then right, then look for number eleven," said Mr. Penderwick, starting up the car.

"What's this Arundel he was talking about?" said Skye.

"And who's Mrs. Tifton?" said Jane.

"Hound needs to go to the bathroom," said Batty.

"Soon, honey," said Rosalind. "Daddy, here—go left."

A few moments later, they were turning onto Stafford Street, and then suddenly Mr. Penderwick stopped the car in the middle of the road and everyone stared in amazement. What had the family expected from a rental cottage? A cozy little tumbledown house with a few pots of geraniums in the front yard. Even Harry the Tomato Man's news hadn't changed that. If anyone had thought about it at all, they had figured snooty Mrs. Tifton lived in a cottage next to theirs and grew vegetables in carefully guarded garden plots.

That's not what they saw. What they saw were two tall, elegant stone pillars, with NUMBER ELEVEN carved across one and ARUNDEL across the other. Beyond the pillars was a lane winding off into the distance, with double rows of tall poplars on either side. And past the poplars was a beautifully tended lawn dotted with graceful trees. There was no house in sight.

"Holy bananas," said Skye.

"Cottages don't have front yards like this," said Rosalind. "Daddy, are you sure you remembered the right address?"

"Pretty sure," said Mr. Penderwick.

He turned the car and started slowly down the lane, which wandered on and on, until the Penderwicks thought they would never reach the end. But finally there was one last curve, the poplar trees ended, and Rosalind's fears were realized. "Daddy, that's not a cottage."

"No, I agree. That's a mansion."

And so it was, a huge mansion crouching in the middle of formal gardens. Built from gray stone, it was covered with towers, balconies, terraces, and turrets that jutted every which way. And the gardens! There were fountains and flowering hedges and marble statues, and that was just in the part the Penderwicks could see from the lane.

"The exhausted travelers saw before them a dwelling fit for kings. Cair Paravel! El Dorado! Camelot!" said Jane.

"Too bad we're not kings," said Skye.

"We're still lost," said Rosalind, discouraged.

"Buck up, Rosy," said Mr. Penderwick. "Here comes someone we can ask."

A tall teenage boy pushing a wheelbarrow had appeared from behind a large statue of Cupid and Venus. Mr. Penderwick rolled down his car window, but before he could call out to the boy, a familiar gagging noise came from the very back of the car.

"Hound's going to barf!" shrieked Batty.

The sisters knew the drill. In a flash they flew out and around to the back of the car and dragged poor Hound over to the side of the lane. He threw up on Jane's sneakers.

"Oh, Hound, how could you?" moaned Jane, looking down at her yellow high-tops, but Hound had already wandered off to inspect a bush.

"This isn't as bad as the time he ate pizza out of the garbage can," said Skye.

Batty crouched down to inspect the mess. "There's the map," she said, pointing.

"Don't touch it!" Rosalind exclaimed. "And, Jane, stop shaking your sneakers. You're splashing it around. Stand still, everyone, until I get back." She ran over to the car for paper towels.

The teenager with the wheelbarrow had come over to the driveway, and Mr. Penderwick had gotten out of the car and was talking to him. "I see there's some *Linnaea borealis* here along the drive. Odd place for it. But I'm particularly interested in *Cypripedium arietinum,* if you know of any good places to hunt for it. It likes swampy land, some shade. . . ."

Rosalind ducked her head into the back of the car and rooted around among the luggage. Her father was talking in Latin about plants, which meant he was happy. She hoped he remembered to ask the boy about directions, too. He looked nice, that boy. Eighteen or maybe nineteen years old, with light brown hair sticking out from under a Red Sox baseball cap. Rosalind peered around the car and sneaked a look at the boy's hands. Her best friend, Anna, always said that you could tell a lot about people from their hands. The boy was wearing gardening gloves.

The paper towels were behind Mr. Penderwick's computer and under a soccer ball. Rosalind grabbed a bunch and rushed back to her sisters. Jane and Skye were piling leaves on top of Hound's barf.

"Remember when he ate that lemon cream pie off the Geigers' picnic table? He really puked that time," said Skye.

"What about when he stole a whole meat loaf out of the refrigerator? He was sick for two days," said Jane.

"Shh," said Rosalind, wiping Jane's sneakers clean. Mr. Penderwick and that boy were walking over.

"Girls, this is Cagney," said Mr. Penderwick.

"Hi," said Cagney, with a big smile. He slipped off his gloves and stuck them in his jeans pocket. Rosalind looked hard at his hands, but they were just regular old hands to her. She wished Anna were there.

"Cagney, these four are my pride and joy. The one with blond hair is my second daughter, Skye—"

"Blue Skye, blue eyes," said Skye, opening wide her blue eyes to demonstrate.

"That's how you can remember which one she is," said Jane. "Blue eyes and straight blond hair. The rest of us have identical brown eyes and dark curly hair. People get me and Rosalind mixed up all the time."

"They do not. I'm much taller than you are," said Rosalind, painfully aware that not only was she holding vomity paper towels, she was wearing her shirt with Wildwood Elementary School across the front. Why had she worn it? She didn't want people to think she was still in elementary school. She was going to start seventh grade in September.

"Yes, well, the tall one is Rosalind, my oldest, the short one is Jane, and—" Mr. Penderwick looked around him.

"Over there," said Jane, pointing to the orange-and-black wings sticking out from behind a tree.

"And that's Batty, the shy one. Now, troops, good news. This is the right place after all. Cagney's the gardener here at Arundel Hall—that's what this mansion is called—and he's been expecting us. Our cottage is at the back of the estate grounds."

"It used to be the guest cottage for the main house," said Cagney. "Back in the days when General and Mrs. Framley were alive. It's quieter here now with Mrs. Tifton in charge."

"Mrs. Tifton!" exclaimed Jane, and would have said more if Rosalind had not dug an elbow into her ribs.

"Okay, girls, let's be off," said Mr. Penderwick. "And Cagney, let's have that talk about the native flora sometime soon."

"Yes, I'd like that," said Cagney. "Now, to get to the cottage, take the driveway up there on the left, and

12

follow it past the carriage house and into the formal gardens. You'll see the sunken garden to your left and the Greek pavilion to the right, and then you'll drive through the boundary hedge. The cottage is a few hundred more yards along. It's yellow. You can't miss it. And the key is under the mat."

Rosalind rounded up Batty, Skye fetched Hound, and soon everyone was in the car ready to go, except for Jane. She was standing in the driveway, staring up at Arundel Hall.

Rosalind leaned out the window. "Jane, come on."

Jane reluctantly turned away from the mansion. "I thought I saw a boy in that window up there. He was looking down at us."

Skye leaned across Batty, flattening her, and looked out Jane's window. "Where?"

"Up there," said Jane, pointing. "Top row, on the right."

"No one's there," said Skye.

"Get off me," said Batty.

Skye settled back into her own seat. "You imagined him, Jane."

"Maybe. I don't think so," said Jane. "But whether I did or not, he's given me a good idea."

CHAPTER TWO
A Tunnel Through the Hedge

ARUNDEL COTTAGE WAS NOT ONLY YELLOW, it was the creamiest, butteriest yellow the Penderwicks had ever seen. It was all a cottage is supposed to be, small and snug, with a front porch, pink climbing roses, and lots of trees for shade.

The key was under the doormat just as Cagney had said it would be. Mr. Penderwick unlocked the door and the family piled through. If possible, the inside of the cottage was even more charming than the outside, all in pretty shades of blues and greens and with the comfortable kind of furniture too sturdy to damage unless you try. Off the living room was a cozy study with a big desk and a sleeping couch, which Mr. Penderwick immediately claimed for himself, saying he wanted to be as far as possible from the madding crowd.

Now it was time for the sisters to go upstairs and choose their bedrooms.

"Dibs first choice." Skye headed toward the steps with her suitcase.

"No fair!" said Jane. "I hadn't thought of it yet."

"Right. I thought of it first, which is why I get first choice," said Skye, already halfway up to the second floor.

"Come back, Skye," said Rosalind. "Hound draws for order."

Skye groaned and reluctantly came back downstairs. She hated leaving important things up to Hound, and besides, he usually drew her last.

The Hound Draw for Order was a time-honored ritual with the sisters. Names were written on small pieces of paper, then dropped on the ground along with broken bits of dog biscuit. As Hound snuffled among the biscuit pieces, he couldn't help but knock into the papers. The person whose paper his big nose hit first was given first choice. Second hit, second choice, and so on.

Rosalind and Jane readied the slips of paper, Batty crumbled a dog biscuit, and Skye held Hound, whispering her name over and over in his ear, trying to hypnotize him. Her efforts were useless. Once let go, he touched Jane's paper first, then Rosalind's, and then Batty's. Skye's piece of paper he ate along with the last piece of biscuit.

"Great," said Skye sadly. "I've got fourth choice and Hound's going to throw up again."

Jane, Batty, and Rosalind flew up the steps with their suitcases to stake their claims on bedrooms. Skye sat downstairs and fretted. She'd been looking forward to picking out a special bedroom, painted white maybe, which she could keep neat and organized. Once upon a time, many years ago, she had slept in a room like that. But then Batty was born and put into Jane's room, and Jane moved in with Skye, and suddenly half of Skye's bedroom was painted lavender and filled with Jane's dolls and books and untidy piles of paper. Even that wouldn't have been so bad if the dolls and papers weren't always drifting over to Skye's side of the room. It had driven Skye crazy and, since Jane had gotten no neater over time, still did. And now, on vacation, Skye had the last pick and would probably end up in some dark, ugly closet. Life was unfair.

Rosalind was calling from upstairs. "Skye, we've all chosen. Come see your bedroom."

Skye dragged herself up the stairs and down the hall to the bedroom Rosalind pointed out. She walked in and was so surprised she let her suitcase fall to the floor with a loud thump. This was no dark, ugly closet.

Her sisters had left her the most perfect bedroom Skye had ever seen. The room was large and white and sparkling clean, with polished wood floors and three windows. And two beds! A whole extra bed without a sister to go along with it!

She wouldn't change a thing about the room, Skye decided. She would leave her stuff in her suitcase, and store the suitcase in the closet, and keep the dresser top bare and the bookshelf empty. No dolls, no combs and brushes, no notebooks full of Sabrina Starr stories. And she would use both beds, sleeping in one on Mondays, Wednesdays, and Fridays and in the other on Tuesdays, Thursdays, and Saturdays. Sunday nights she would have to switch in the middle of the night.

Skye opened her suitcase, pulled out a math book—she was teaching herself algebra for fun—and wrote the bed schedule next to her favorite word problem about trains traveling in different directions. Next she rummaged around for her lucky camouflage hat, the one she'd been wearing when she fell off the garage roof and didn't break any arms or legs. There it was, under her black T-shirts. Skye crammed the hat onto her head and closed the suitcase and shoved it into the closet.

"Now for exploring," she said, and, after one more long, satisfied look at her glorious bedroom, left in search of her sisters.

Rosalind was down the hall in a small bedroom—with only one window and one bed—neatly transferring clothes from her suitcase to dresser drawers.

"You gave me the better room," said Skye.

"I wanted to be near Batty," said Rosalind.

"Well, thanks," said Skye, who knew that Rosalind would have loved the luxury of a large bedroom.

Rosalind took a framed picture out of her suitcase and set it on her bedside table. Skye walked over to look, though she already knew the picture by heart—Rosalind kept it beside her bed at home, too, and Skye had seen it a million times. It showed Mrs. Penderwick laughing and hugging little baby Rosalind, still so young that not even Skye had been born yet, let alone Jane or Batty.

It was a strongly held belief among all the Penderwicks that Skye would grow up to look exactly like her mother. All the Penderwicks, that is, except for Skye. She thought her mother the most beautiful woman she had ever seen, and it certainly wasn't beauty that Skye saw when she looked in the mirror. The blond hair and blue eyes were the same, true, but that was it, as far as Skye could tell. And then, of course, there was that other big difference—Skye couldn't imagine herself ever hugging a little baby and laughing at the same time.

Batty burst out of Rosalind's closet, her wings flying behind her.

"I found a secret passage," said Batty.

Skye looked into the closet and saw straight through into another bedroom exactly like Rosalind's, but with Batty's suitcase lying open on the bed. "It's not a secret passage. It's a closet between two bedrooms."

"It is a secret passage. And you can't use it."

Skye turned her back on Batty and said to Rosalind, "I'm going exploring. Do you want to come?"

"Not now, I'm still getting settled. Can Batty go with you?" said Rosalind.

"No," said Skye and Batty together. Skye left before Rosalind could try to change anyone's mind.

Jane had staked her claim on the third floor, which was really the attic. Skye skipped up a steep flight of steps and discovered her younger sister perched on a narrow brass bed, writing furiously in a blue notebook and muttering to herself. "The boy Arthur shook the iron bars and raged against his wicked kidnapper—no, that's too dramatic. How about, Arthur stared sadly—no—the *lonely* boy named Arthur stared sadly out the window, never dreaming that help was on the way. Oh, that's a good sentence. Unknown to him, the great Sabrina—"

Skye interrupted her. "I'm going exploring. Do you want to come?"

Her eyes shining, Jane said, "Look at this wonderful bedroom. It was meant for an author. I know I can

19

write the perfect Sabrina Starr book here. I can feel it. Can you feel it?"

Skye looked around the tiny room with its sloped ceiling and one round window high on the wall. Already there were books all over the floor. "No. I don't feel anything."

"Oh, try harder. The feeling is so strong. I'm sure that some famous writer has been here before me. Like Louisa May Alcott or Patricia MacLachlan."

"Jane, do you want to come with me or not?"

"Not now. I have to write down some ideas for my book. I might have Sabrina Starr rescue an actual person in this book. A boy. What do you think?"

"I didn't think she could even rescue a groundhog," said Skye, but Jane was already writing again.

Skye ran down two flights of steps and outside. She found her father getting Hound settled in his pen. It was, to Skye's eyes, a sort of doggy paradise. The metal fence was tall—and Hound didn't like fences—but the pen was large, and inside it were trees for shade, sticks for chewing, and a patch of dirt for digging. Plus Mr. Penderwick had put out a huge bowl of Hound's favorite food and two bowls of fresh water. Hound, however, wasn't grateful. When he saw Skye, he rushed the gate, barking and whining as though he was being locked up in a dungeon.

"Be still, demon dog," said Mr. Penderwick.

"He's trying to open the gate," said Skye, watching Hound poke and prod with his nose at the metal latch.

"That latch is dog-proof. He'll be safe in here."

Skye reached through the fence and scratched Hound's nose. "Daddy, I'm going exploring. Is that okay?"

"As long as you're back in an hour for dinner. And Skye, *quidquid agas prudenter agas et respice finem.*"

Mr. Penderwick didn't use Latin just for plants, but in his everyday speech, too. He said that it kept his brain properly exercised. Much of the time his daughters had no idea what he was talking about, but Skye was used to hearing this phrase, which Mr. Penderwick translated loosely as "look before you leap and please don't do anything crazy."

"Don't worry, Daddy," she said, and meant it. Sneaking into that Mrs. Tifton's gardens, which is what Skye planned to do, wasn't crazy. On the other hand, it wasn't the most correct thing—according to Harry the Tomato Man—but maybe he'd been wrong. Maybe Mrs. Tifton loved having strangers wandering around her gardens. After all, anything's possible, thought Skye, and off she went, waving good-bye to her father and Hound.

The land surrounding the cottage was large enough for three or four soccer fields. Not that anyone could play a normal game of soccer there, thought Skye—

21

too many trees. They grew thickest behind the cottage, and the spaces between were filled with nasty, thorny underbrush. The land in front was much more inviting. Here the trees were farther apart, and pretty grasses and wildflowers grew among them.

On one side of the property, a high stone wall separated the cottage from its neighbors. Along the front and the other side ran a boundary hedge. Skye knew that Mrs. Tifton's gardens were beyond that hedge. She had two options for getting there. She could walk back up the driveway and through the break in the hedge. Boring, and likely to lead to being caught—it's hard to hide on a driveway. Or she could crawl through the hedge and emerge in some sheltered garden nook where neither Mrs. Tifton nor anyone else would be likely to see her.

Definitely option two, Skye decided, veering away from the driveway and toward the hedge. But she found the hedge to be thicker and more prickly than she had anticipated, and after several attempts to crawl through, she had accomplished nothing except snagging her hat twice and scratching her arms until it looked like she had fought a tiger.

Then, when she was just about to give up and go around by the driveway, she discovered a way in. It was a tunnel, carefully hidden behind a clump of tall wildflowers and just the right size for going through on all fours. Now, if Rosalind had been the first to discover that tunnel, she would have noticed that it was too neatly trimmed and pricker-free to be there by mistake, and she would have figured that someone used it often and that the someone probably wasn't Mrs. Tifton. If Jane had been the first, she, too, would have realized that natural forces hadn't formed that tunnel. Her explanation for it would have been nonsense—an escape route for convicts on the run or talking badgers—but at least she would have thought about it. But this was Skye. She only thought, I need a way through the hedge, and here it is. And then she plunged.

She emerged on the edge of the enormous formal gardens, directly behind a marble statue of a man wrapped in a bedsheet and holding a thunderbolt over his head. It seemed to Skye a ridiculous thing to put in a garden, but she was glad for the cover. She peered around the marble man—she was in luck. There was only one person in sight, pulling weeds from between flagstones, and he was already a friend.

"Cagney," she called out, and ran over to him, lifting her hat to show him her blond hair. "It's me, Skye Penderwick."

"Blue Skye, blue—" he started to say but was cut off, because now someone else was shouting his name. Someone who was close by and coming closer. "I'd better hide you. Sounds like she's in a bad mood."

"Who?" asked Skye, but Cagney was already lifting her right off the ground and into a large urn carved all over with vines and flowers.

"Keep your head low and stay quiet till she's gone."

Skye crouched down and wished that Cagney had put her into an urn that didn't have three inches of dirty water at the bottom, but there wasn't time to worry about that, because the person in a bad mood was coming closer still, and now Cagney was calling out, "Over here, Mrs. Tifton!"

Skye froze—the mysterious Mrs. Tifton! If only Skye could see! Why didn't urns have spy holes in them?

"For heaven's sake, Cagney, didn't you hear me calling? I don't have time to be hunting you down." The voice was sharp and impatient. It reminded Skye of her second-grade teacher, the one who'd accused her of cheating when she did long division, because second graders were only supposed to add and subtract. Along with the unpleasant voice came an annoying tap tap tapping noise on the flagstones. Mrs. Tifton must be wearing high heels. Snooty high heels.

"Yes, ma'am, I'm sorry, ma'am. It won't happen again, ma'am," said Cagney.

"I've just received the schedule for the Garden Club competition. The judge and the committee will be here at Arundel three Mondays from now. You know they'll be looking at gardens all over Massachusetts. I want mine to win this year."

"It will, Mrs. Tifton. I promise."

"You still have a lot of work to do."

"Yes, ma'am."

"What are you going to do with these urns? They look ridiculous empty."

To Skye's horror, the tap tap tapping noise was now heading toward her. She scrunched down even lower and was glad, at least, for her camouflage hat. It might hide her from above, if Mrs. Tifton was half blind.

Suddenly there was a big thump, and Skye rocked back and forth in her hiding place. Cagney had taken a great leap in front of Mrs. Tifton and landed against the urn.

"Jasmine," he said. "Lots of pink jasmine from the greenhouse. Would you like to go see it now? Help me select the best plants?"

"Of course not. That's what I pay you for. Oh, and Cagney, I want you to cut down that big white rosebush next to the driveway."

"The Fimbriata?" To Skye, Cagney's voice sounded the same as her father's had the day Hound ate a rare orchid.

"It scratched Mrs. Robinette's car after the last Garden Club committee meeting. Get rid of it."

"Yes, ma'am."

25

When Mrs. Tifton's high heels had faded off into the distance, Skye felt safe enough to look up. Cagney was staring down at her gloomily. He said, "My uncle planted that rose thirty years ago. He wrapped it in burlap every winter to keep it alive. I can't kill it now just because Mrs. Robinette doesn't know how to steer." He lifted Skye out of the urn.

"Your uncle was a gardener here, too?" said Skye.

"Uh-huh. I started coming over after school to help him when I was younger than you. He retired last year, and Mrs. Tifton gave me his job."

Skye bounced up and down to squish the dirty water out of her sneakers, then had a thought. "Why not move that rose over to our cottage? Daddy can take care of it while we're here."

Cagney brightened. "I could do that. Mrs. Tifton would never know. And I wouldn't need to bother your father. I'll come over to water it every day."

Then came that voice again, from far away. "Caagneey!"

"Here we go again," said Cagney. "You'd better get out of here. I'll head her off before she sees you."

Although Skye would have preferred getting into the urn and spying on Mrs. Tifton again, she knew Cagney was right. She shook his hand good-bye, then, dodging from bush to bush, made her way around to the back of the marble thunderbolt man.

"Caagneey," she heard again, closer. Skye hurled herself into the hedge tunnel and—*CRASH!*—slammed into someone and fell to the ground in a tangle of arms and legs.

"Ouch!" She checked her head for blood. But the camouflage hat had softened the blow and there was no major damage. Which was good, because she'd still have the strength to murder whichever of her sisters had caused this accident. She untwisted herself, pushed her hair out of her eyes, and looked at the person lying half under her.

It wasn't one of her sisters. It was a boy about her own age with freckles and straight brown hair. His eyes were closed, and he was pale and lying still.

"Are you unconscious?" said Skye in a panic. She yanked off her hat and fanned him with it. She had seen a cowboy use his hat to revive another cowboy in a movie once. But it wasn't working—the boy's eyes didn't open. Sometimes in movies they slap people, she thought, but she hesitated to slap someone she had just knocked out. Still, the boy was in trouble. If she had to slap him, she had to. She pulled back her hand and—

He opened his eyes.

"Thank goodness," said Skye. "I thought you were dying."

"Not yet."

"Does your head hurt?"

He touched his forehead and winced. "Not too bad."

"Okay, good. I'm going to help you get home. Where do you live?"

"I live—"

"JEFFREY!" It was Mrs. Tifton's voice again, and she sounded very close now.

Skye put her hand over the boy's mouth and whispered, "Shh, trouble. That's snooty Mrs. Tifton and she's a real pain. If she caught us in her gardens, she'd—"

The boy jerked away from her hand and struggled to sit up. He was even more pale than before, so pale she could count every freckle on his face.

"Are you all right? You look like you're going to be sick," she said.

"JEFFREY! Where are you?" came Mrs. Tifton's voice again.

Then Skye finally understood. "Oh, no."

"Excuse me," said the boy with great dignity. "My mother's calling me and you're in my way."

CHAPTER THREE
The MOOPS

IT WAS BATTY'S BEDTIME. She had taken a bath, brushed her teeth, and put on her mermaid pajamas, and now she was standing in the middle of her Arundel bedroom, looking around. The butterfly wings were hanging on the closet doorknob, ready for morning. Her favorite picture of Hound, the one that her father had framed, was on the little white dresser by the window. Rosalind had put Batty's special unicorn blanket on the bed, and Sedgewick the horse, Funty the blue elephant, Ursula the bear, and Fred the other bear were sitting on the pillow. It was an okay bedroom, Batty decided, not as safe and cozy as her room at home, but at least the closet had that secret passage into Rosalind's room. Nothing scary could hide in a closet like that, not with Rosalind right there.

Rosalind would be along in a minute to tell Batty a story. She came every night, just as every night Daddy came after the story to tuck Batty in and kiss her good night. Batty thought that she'd like the story tonight to be about her mother. She had heard Rosalind's stories about Mrs. Penderwick many, many times, but that didn't make them any less wonderful, especially when the only place to go to sleep afterward was a strange and unfamiliar bed.

Batty sat on the edge of the bed and bounced. It felt all right, she guessed. She wouldn't mind so much about it being strange if Hound could sleep with her or if Rosalind was going to be in the room next door right away. But Hound was never allowed to sleep in the bedrooms because he insisted on licking faces in the middle of the night. And Rosalind wouldn't be going to her room for a while, because Skye had called for a MOOPS at eight o'clock. A MOOPS was a Meeting Of Older Penderwick Sisters. Rosalind, Skye, and Jane called it MOOPS to keep Mr. Penderwick from knowing what they were talking about. Batty wasn't supposed to know either, but she knew about MOPS, which was a Meeting Of Penderwick Sisters, because she was always invited to them. And MOOPS had only one more letter. Skye had spelled it out, em-oh-oh-pee-ess, as though that would keep Batty from knowing what it was. Batty swung her feet back and forth and wished Skye didn't always leave her out of things.

The door to Batty's bedroom swung open, and Hound slipped through, his tail wagging wildly.

"Hound!" cried Batty. "How did you get up here?"

There was no time for talk. Rosalind would be along soon. Batty shoved Hound into the closet and shut the door behind him. Later, she would let him out and they could hold their own meeting and not invite anyone else. Batty jumped back onto the bed to wait for Rosalind.

But when someone came in through her bedroom door a minute later, it wasn't Rosalind. It was Hound all over again, looking pleased with himself.

"Hound!" cried Batty again, but this time with despair. He must have taken the secret passage and come all the way around. She dashed into the closet, shut the door into Rosalind's room, and was trying to drag Hound back into hiding when Rosalind arrived.

"It's all right," said Rosalind. "Daddy's letting Hound stay up here with you for a special treat. We thought you might be worried about sleeping alone in a new room."

"I'm not worried."

"Just remember, he's not allowed on the bed."

"Okay," Batty said, and let go of Hound. He ran across the room and jumped onto the bed.

Rosalind pushed him back down to the floor and asked Batty, "Have you picked your story yet?"

Batty slid in between the sheets. The bed suddenly seemed more welcoming now that Hound was going to be there all night. "Tell me how Mommy gave me my name."

Rosalind would rather have told a different story, one from when Mrs. Penderwick was younger and not so close to dying. But she knew this was one of Batty's favorites. After all, there were so few stories about Batty and her mother together. Rosalind sat on the bed next to Batty and began, "Right after you were born, Daddy and I visited you and Mommy in the hospital."

"But Skye and Jane weren't there," said Batty with great satisfaction.

"Right. Aunt Claire was staying with us to help out, and Skye and Jane were home with her. Mommy was sitting up in the hospital bed and wearing a beautiful blue robe and cuddling you in her arms. Daddy asked, 'What should we name her, darling?' and Mommy said, 'Name her after me.'"

"Then Daddy got sad."

"That's right. Daddy got sad and said there could only ever be one Elizabeth for him. So Mommy said, 'Then name her Elizabeth, but call her Batty. I think she has a sense of humor.'"

"And then I smiled."

"And Mommy said, 'You see, Martin? She's smiling. She likes it. Don't you, Batty?' And she kissed you and you smiled again."

"Then two weeks later, Mommy died from cancer and I came home from the hospital."

"Yes." Rosalind turned her head away so that Batty couldn't see the sadness in her face.

"And you called me Beautiful Baby Batty, and Skye and Jane called me Banana Batty."

"And we all lived happily ever after. Now go to sleep. Daddy will be up in a minute," Rosalind finished. She straightened Batty's covers, kissed her forehead, and turned out the room light. As she was closing the door on her way out, she heard a big thump and knew that Hound had jumped back onto the bed. She sighed, then headed down the hallway toward Skye's bedroom. It was time for the MOOPS.

"I thought you'd never get here," said Jane when Rosalind opened the door. "Skye won't give me any hints about the MOOPS topic, and she keeps trying to explain irrational numbers to me. I don't need that stuff until at least seventh grade."

"You won't get anywhere in life with that attitude," said Skye.

"That's enough, Skye," said Rosalind, and sat on the Tuesday-Thursday-Saturday bed with Jane. Skye was on the Monday-Wednesday-Friday bed, facing them. "MOOPS come to order."

33

"Second the motion," said Skye.

"Third it," said Jane, bouncing excitedly.

"All swear to keep secret what is said here, even from Daddy, unless you think someone might do something truly bad," said Rosalind, with a particular look at Skye, who ignored her. Rosalind made her right hand into a fist and held it out toward her sisters. Skye put her fist on top of Rosalind's, and Jane put hers on top of Skye's.

In unison, they chanted, "This I swear, by the Penderwick Family Honor," then broke their fists apart.

"Okay, Skye, now tell!" said Jane.

Skye leaned forward and whispered, "I got into those gardens."

"You called a MOOPS for that?" said Jane. "That's no big deal. I'm going to sneak in there tomorrow."

"Let me finish. I met that Mrs. Tifton. That is, I heard her talking. I couldn't actually meet her, because Cagney had just stuck me into an urn."

"Oh, Skye, what were you up to?" moaned Rosalind.

Skye hurried on. "But that's not what I need to tell you. There's a boy over there, I mean besides Cagney. A boy my age."

"Oh!" said Jane. "So I did see a boy at the window."

"What?" asked Skye.

"Earlier today, when we drove up, I saw a boy watching us from a window in the mansion. I told you that," said Jane.

"You said you imagined him," said Skye.

"No, *you* said I imagined him. And *I* said that I didn't think so, and it looks like I didn't, right?"

"One of these days, Jane, you're going to send me right over the edge," said Skye.

"All right, Skye," said Rosalind. "Did you talk to this boy?"

"Yes," Skye said, and shut her mouth like a trap.

"What happened?"

"Nothing."

"Skye!"

"All right!" said Skye. "We crashed into each other and he seemed like he was knocked out, but then he woke up and I figured he was some kid from the neighborhood, so I said some bad things about Mrs. Tifton and upset him. It wasn't my fault. I had just hit my head—maybe I had a little concussion. How could I know who he was? My wacko sister Jane doesn't know reality from fantasy, and Harry the Tomato Man didn't say anything about a son, and neither did Cagney."

"A son?" asked Rosalind.

"This kid—his name is Jeffrey—is Mrs. Tifton's son."

"Her son!" said Jane. "Oh, my!"

"Well, what happened? Did you straighten it all out?" asked Rosalind.

"No. She was yelling for him, and he left," said Skye.

"You've got to apologize to him," said Rosalind.

"I can't, I can't. I'm too embarrassed."

"Then one of us has to apologize for you, for the family honor."

"I will," said Jane eagerly.

"Oh, no, you won't!" said Skye. "You'll start babbling about Sabrina Starr and he'll think we're all fruitcakes."

"He probably already thinks that after meeting you," said Jane.

"Rosalind, please, you do it," said Skye.

Rosalind looked gravely at her two younger sisters. Skye was right, she thought. No one ever knew what Jane would say once her imagination took hold. On the other hand, maybe it was time Rosalind stopped bailing Skye out. "I vote that Jane apologize to this boy," she said slowly.

"Two votes to one," crowed Jane, while Skye slapped her hand to her forehead like she had just gotten a terrible headache.

"But—" said Rosalind, and Skye looked at her, hopeful. "But we all decide everything together ahead of time. No wild flights of fantasy."

"No fantasy at all," added Skye.

"I promise," said Jane.

"And we have to tell Daddy beforehand," said Rosalind.

"Can we leave out the stuff I said about Mrs.

Tifton?" pleaded Skye. "I'll give you my next week's allowance."

"Bribery is immoral," Rosalind said sternly.

"I'll take your allowance," said Jane.

"Why should you—" said Skye.

"Order!" Rosalind pounded her fist on the bed. "There will be no exchange of money. Skye, I'll let you decide how much to tell Daddy, as long as you do it before Jane goes over there."

"Thank you," said Skye.

"You're welcome," said Rosalind. "Now, Jane, here's what you'll say to Jeffrey. . . ."

CHAPTER FOUR
The Apology

"**W**HY CAN'T WE GIVE THAT BOY regular old cookies from the supermarket?" said Skye, poking at a bowl of batter with a wooden spoon. She and Rosalind were in the kitchen, making cookies for Jeffrey. Jane had left a few minutes earlier for Arundel Hall to deliver the apology, soothe Jeffrey's wounded feelings, and try to bring him back to the cottage for an apology party.

"Don't attack the batter. Stir the way Mommy taught us," said Rosalind.

"I don't remember anything about stirring. I remember Mommy singing that song about all the little chocolate chips goin' to cookie heaven and I remember putting batter in Jane's hair."

Rosalind took the bowl and spoon, demonstrated how to stir, then handed them back.

"You know Jane's going to mess it all up. Jeffrey will get more upset and hate all of us instead of just me. This cookie thing is a waste of time," said Skye with an only slightly improved stirring method.

"Jane will do fine."

"Even if she does, he won't accept the apology. Why should he? I wouldn't if someone said that kind of stuff about Daddy."

"Nobody would say anything bad about Daddy," said Rosalind, then looked out the window to see why Hound was barking. It was Cagney, pulling up in a pickup truck. "What do you think Cagney's doing here? He's got a big bush in a truck."

"It must be the rescued rose. Cagney scores one, Mrs. Tifton zero."

"I'll see if he needs any help with it." Rosalind took off her apron and smoothed back her hair.

"Rosalind, wait! Don't leave me here alone—I don't know what to do next."

"Use a teaspoon to drop the batter onto the cookie sheets, then put them in the oven. Don't panic. I'll be back in a few minutes," said Rosalind, slipping out the door. She found Cagney at Hound's pen, rubbing Hound's ears and trying to get Batty to say hello to him. A minute before, Batty had been playing ballerinas with Hound, but now she was standing very still, being invisible.

"Good morning," said Rosalind to Cagney.

"Rosalind, right?"

Rosalind nodded, pleased he had remembered.

"Your little sister won't talk to me."

"She never does with new people. She waits until she's found a common interest."

Cagney leaned over and whispered to Rosalind. "What about rabbits?"

"She loves rabbits," Rosalind whispered back.

"I have two living with me."

"Oh, Batty, Cagney has two rabbits," said Rosalind.

Batty's eyes grew big with wonder and she forgot to be invisible.

"Bring her over sometime to meet them," said Cagney. "I live in the carriage house next to Arundel Hall."

Rosalind suddenly felt as shy as Batty. She turned toward the truck and asked, "Where are you going to put the bush?"

"Over there," he said, pointing. "In that sunny spot by the porch."

"I'll get it for you." Rosalind jumped onto the back bumper of the truck, wrapped her arms around the bush, and shrieked as a dozen thorns dug into her skin. Now, Rosalind had never cared about plants. She had wanted to for her father's sake, but in her secret heart, a plant was just one more thing that needed feeding and coddling. Even so, she should have remembered that roses have thorns. She was the practical Penderwick. And practical people, she thought, shouldn't go all silly and forgetful around handsome teenage boys. She knew what her friend Anna would say about it: The cuter the boy, the mushier your brain.

"I do that all the time. Hurts, doesn't it?" said Cagney.

"It's not too bad."

Cagney helped her off the back of the truck, then lifted the rosebush down himself.

"You grab the shovel," he said. "We'll plant it together."

While Rosalind tussled with the rosebush, Jane marched steadily along the driveway toward Arundel Hall. No sneaking through the hedge tunnel, Rosalind had said. Jane must go the long way around and show herself honestly.

"Good morning, Mrs. Tifton," she recited as she went. She was practicing one of the two speeches prepared at last night's MOOPS. "I'm Jane Penderwick, daughter of Martin Penderwick, who is renting Arundel Cottage. Please, may I speak with Jeffrey?" Jane hoped that she wouldn't meet Mrs. Tifton and then she wouldn't have to use this speech. Who knew what the boy Jeffrey had told his mother? She might already be disgusted with Penderwicks.

Jane began the other speech. "Good morning, Jeffrey. I'm Jane Penderwick, officially elected spokesperson for Skye Penderwick, whom you met yesterday, to your own sorrow. Whoops." Skye had sworn she'd kill Jane if she kept in the part about sorrow, but it sounded so romantic that Jane kept wanting to say it, anyway.

Jane followed the driveway as it cut through the big hedge and curved through the formal gardens. There it was, Arundel Hall. She slowed her steps, nervously beginning the Jeffrey speech again. "Good morning, Jeffrey. I'm Jane Penderwick, elected spokesperson for Skye Penderwick, whom you met yesterday, to your—to your not anything. Skye asked me to express her regret at—oh, nuts, what was the rest?"

Jane was now close enough to the mansion to look up at the window where she had seen Jeffrey the day before. She had been hoping he would be there again, and she could wave to him and maybe he would come down for her speech. But today the window was empty. She was going to have to knock on one of the mansion's doors. There had been much discussion at the MOOPS about which door to choose. The fancy carved oak door at the front had been rejected as the most likely to have Mrs. Tifton behind it. But that still left a lot of doors. The sisters had noticed at least three or four, and that was just in the parts of the mansion they'd driven by. In the end, Rosalind had said that

Jane should look for the simplest door she could find. With any luck, Mrs. Tifton wouldn't open a simple door.

Jane circled the mansion, passing door after door, all too la-di-da for comfort. Until, all the way around at the back of Arundel Hall, she came to a plain green door with a shiny brass doorbell and a mat that said WELCOME. Jane said, "Sabrina Starr surveyed the scene. She saw nothing dangerous. Could it be a trap? But who cares about danger when there's an assignment to carry out?"

She rang the doorbell.

"Hold on," a woman's voice called from inside the house.

Jane muttered under her breath, "Good morning, Mrs. Tifton. I'm Jane Penderwick, daughter of Arundel Cottage. No, oh, no, no, daughter of Martin—"

The door opened and a plump woman with short gray hair looked out at Jane. This couldn't be Mrs. Tifton, thought Jane. No one would ever call this woman snooty. Comfortable, that's what people would call her.

"What a relief," said Jane. "For although Sabrina Starr had enough courage to face her adversaries, it was nicer when she didn't have to."

"And you are?" said the woman, who didn't look at all put out by Sabrina Starr. Jane decided on the spot to like her.

43

"Jane Penderwick."

"From the cottage. Cagney told me your family had arrived. A professor and a lot of girls, he said."

"And Hound."

"Oh, yes, the dog we're keeping secret from Mrs. Tifton."

"She doesn't like dogs?"

"Let's just say that your Hound doesn't sound like her type. By the way, I'm Mrs. Churchill, the house-keeper here, but everyone calls me Churchie. Would you like to come in?"

More than anything, Jane would have liked to go inside. There was some wonderful baking smell float-ing out the door, and probably Churchie would offer Jane whatever it was that smelled so good and they could have a cozy chat about the Tiftons, and maybe Churchie would even give Jane a tour. But now was not the time for frivolity. Jane had a mission to accomplish. She said, "Thank you very much, but per-haps another time. I need to speak with Jeffrey. Is he here?"

"Hang on," Churchie said, and disappeared back into the mansion.

Jane had been concentrating too hard on memoriz-ing speeches to have time to wonder what Jeffrey looked like. Skye had said nothing about it, and Jane's own glimpse of him had been too brief and from too far away to get much of an idea. On the other hand, Jane knew exactly how Arthur, the boy in her new Sabrina Starr book, was going to look. He would have tawny eyes like a lion, and dark auburn curls, and a sad but noble expression brought on by his years of suffering. All who saw him would love him and sing praises to the goodness of his nature, such as—

"Hello," said a boy's voice.

Jane's eyes flew open (she had closed them to better picture Arthur). Right in front of her was a real boy to look at. He didn't have tawny eyes and auburn hair, but Jane all of a sudden understood that brown hair and green eyes could be nice. And if his face had too many freckles to be called noble, still, she already knew he wasn't the kind of boy to tell tales to his mother.

"How's your head?" she asked.

He leaned down a bit to give her a better view of the purple bruise on his forehead. "It's okay. Churchie put ice on it when I got home."

"Good." Jane beamed, then pulled herself together. She still hadn't done her job. "I have a speech for you."

Churchie came up behind Jeffrey. "Sure you don't want to come in, Jane?"

"She has a speech," said Jeffrey.

"Heavens!" said Churchie.

"You can listen if you'd like," offered Jane.

"How could I pass it up?"

Jane cleared her throat, stood tall with her hands

45

clasped behind her back, and began. "Good morning, Jeffrey. I'm Jane Penderwick, officially elected spokesperson for Skye Penderwick, whom you met yesterday. Skye asked me to express her regret for crashing into you and for her subsequent rude behavior and hopes you will forgive her and not take it too personally. The end." Jane bowed.

Churchie applauded. "We don't get many speeches here. That was a good one. What do you think, Jeffrey?"

"It was fine," he said. "I accept the apology."

"Already?" said Jane. "I figured you'd need persuading, so I've been thinking up more things to say. Like how Skye's always saying exactly the wrong thing to people—it wasn't just special for you. And how she's really nice, sometimes, after you get to know her. And then I'd ask you to have pity on motherless girls brought up without a woman's gentle influence, which doesn't really count, because our father is gentle, but I thought it sounded good. I have more, too, if none of that worked."

"You can stop," said Jeffrey. "Not that it wasn't great."

"Yes, very well put," said Churchie.

"Thanks!" Jane hadn't been so proud of herself since delivering the speech for the dedication of the new playground at Wildwood Elementary School. And in a minute she was even prouder, for Jeffrey agreed to go back with her to the cottage for homemade chocolate chip cookies. She had done it! She had soothed the wounded pride of the former enemy and was about to deliver him to the Penderwick camp! Not even Rosalind could have done better.

Jane said good-bye to Churchie, and the two children set off for the cottage, talking a mile a minute. For, to Jane's delight, Jeffrey seemed to like to talk almost as much as she did. This gave her a chance to do some research for her book. She had been having trouble deciding what Arthur would talk about, except imprisonment and doom, of course, and imprisonment and doom can only go so far. Jeffrey seemed willing to talk about anything. He told Jane about watching her family arrive from his window, but his mother had called him just as they were getting back into the car—that's why he had disappeared suddenly. And Jane told him about Hound throwing up in the driveway and how nice Cagney had been about it. And Jeffrey told her about how nice Cagney always was and about the stuff he was always doing for Jeffrey, like making a tunnel through the hedge so that Jeffrey could escape from visiting Garden Club ladies and giving him an iguana named Darwin, but Darwin made his mother break out in hives, so he'd had to give it to Churchie's married daughter in Boston. And Jane told him all about the other Penderwicks, and what their names were, and how Rosalind was the prettiest, Skye the smartest, and Batty the littlest. And Jeffrey told her that he was an only child and that it sometimes got lonely. And Jane said, Well, you won't be lonely for the next three weeks, because we'll be here. And he said, That'll be great. And Jane said that they should hurry, because the chocolate chip cookies must be almost done, and everyone would be so pleased to see him.

Because Rosalind didn't come back in a few minutes like she had promised, Skye struggled on her own with the cookie preparation. She finished stirring the batter, tossed little blobs onto the cookie sheets, shoved the cookie sheets into the oven, and turned the knob to broil. Now there was nothing to do but wait and see if Jeffrey showed up. So she went upstairs to her neat white bedroom, pulled her math book out of her suitcase, and forgot all about the cookies.

Which is how it happened that when smoke began to leak out of the oven, no one was there to notice. Mr. Penderwick was where he had been since breakfast, in his room reading about wildflowers. Jane and Jeffrey were still on their way to the cottage. Rosalind was outside with Cagney and the rosebush, and Batty and Hound were in his pen playing astronauts on the moon. Skye? She was working.

"A tree casts a shadow 20 feet long, and a girl who is 5 feet tall casts a shadow of 4 feet. What is the height of the tree? Okay, if the height of the tree is x, then x over 20 is hmmm—" She scribbled enthusiastically in her math book. "—which means that x equals 100 divided by 4, or 25. Easy. No problem. I am the champ. Next. Four gallons of ice cream . . ."

On and on she went, solving problem after problem as more and more smoke poured out of the oven. Nothing broke her concentration, not even the far-away sound of Hound barking danger-danger-danger. It wasn't until she heard doors slamming and lots of running around downstairs that she looked up and sniffed. What *was* that smell? She ran down the steps into the kitchen.

Skye was amazed at what she saw. Rosalind was pulling two smoldering black cookie sheets out of the oven, Cagney was dragging a hose into the kitchen from outside, Batty and Hound were tearing around the table playing firemen, and everywhere there was smoke, smoke, and more smoke.

"What happened?" said Skye.

"You ruined the cookies and almost burnt down the cottage, that's what happened," said Rosalind, coughing. "What made you turn on the broiler? What were you thinking?"

Skye didn't know a broiler from a boiler from a rolling pin, but she was too mortified to admit it in front of Cagney. She put on her most stubborn face. "I wasn't thinking of anything."

"Well, that much is obvious," said Rosalind. "I didn't know you were such a moron in the kitchen."

Rosalind had gone too far. Skye knew it, and she knew that Rosalind knew it, too, by the look on her face. And Skye knew that Rosalind was about to apologize. But it was too late. Skye lost her temper.

"You promised you'd come back inside and help me, and you didn't, so it's your fault as much as mine. Besides, these stupid cookies weren't my idea in the first place. They were your and Jane's idea. I would never make cookies for a boy, especially a rich, stuck-up boy with a snooty mother!"

Suddenly the kitchen was very quiet and no one was looking at Skye. They were all looking the other way, toward the door. Slowly Skye turned her head and saw what she least wanted to see—Jane and Jeffrey, staring in through the screen. And again Jeffrey was so pale Skye could count his freckles.

"Oh, no." Skye wished that the cottage had burnt down and she was at the bottom of a pile of charred rubble.

That's when Mr. Penderwick wandered into the room. "Well, my goodness," he said cheerfully. "Have we had an accident? Good morning, Cagney—quick work with the hose. And is this Jeffrey Tifton? Hello, son, I'm happy to meet you."

CHAPTER FIVE
A New Hero

Mr. PENDERWICK BELIEVED IN LONG WALKS. One of his favorite sayings was, Take a walk, clear your head. Skye figured that's why he had sent her on a walk with Jane, Jeffrey, and Batty while he and Rosalind aired out the kitchen. For Skye to clear her head and, maybe, too, for Skye and Jeffrey to clear the air between them. Not that Skye hadn't already apologized for calling Jeffrey rich and stuck-up and not that Jeffrey hadn't said that was all right, forget about it, but that was as far as they had gotten, conversationally, and since then, they had barely looked at each other.

So here was Skye, slogging along behind Jeffrey and Jane, listening to them gab on and on like old friends. It was enough to make a person sick. Of course, Skye wasn't jealous and she didn't wish anyone would pay attention to her or anything. It was just such a waste of time being with people who talked about boring stuff.

Jeffrey was taking them to see something special, or so he had told Jane. He led them across the cottage grounds away from the hedge and toward the high stone wall that marked the other boundary line. Once they reached the wall, they turned to the left and followed it for another hundred yards until they came to a wooden gate, where Jeffrey called a halt. The gate was almost as high as the wall—much too high to see over—but there were knotholes in the wood. Jeffrey told Jane to put her eye to one of these knotholes and look through to the other side.

"It's just a field," said Jane.

"There should be a bull over there," said Jeffrey.

"Nope, no bull."

"Let me look."

Jane moved aside to make room for Jeffrey.

"You're right. I don't see him, either," he said. "He must be in the barn today."

Skye tapped her foot impatiently. The truth was, she thought, there was no bull. That boy was just trying to impress Jane.

"He gored a man right in this very field," said Jeffrey, looking back at Jane.

"Oh!" gasped Jane. "Did the man die?"

"Almost." If Jeffrey heard Skye's scornful snort, he

52

didn't let on. "Cagney told me all about it. The man's guts fell out of his stomach and it took three doctors to stitch him back up again. Some people signed a petition to have the bull shot, but the police said it was the man's own fault, because he was trespassing in the bull's field."

"I feel sorry for the man, but just the same, it would be awful to be shot," said Jane.

"Besides, Cagney says the bull's more dumb than mean. It's not right to shoot someone because they're not intelligent," said Jeffrey.

"He could be hiding in a corner." Jane looked through the gate again. The knothole was too small to give much of a view.

"There's a ladder in the wall farther down. We could climb it and look over the top," Jeffrey said. He turned and looked at Skye. "Do you want to come?"

Skye didn't, but because she figured that Jeffrey didn't want her, she shrugged and said, "Sure, okay."

So off they went, Jane and Jeffrey talking, talking, talking and Skye trailing behind, wishing she had never gone through that stupid tunnel and bumped into this jerky boy.

Stay close to your sisters, Rosalind had told Batty, and Batty had stayed pretty close while they were all walking, but when Jeffrey stopped at the gate, Batty drifted away and hid behind a bush. Not just because of

53

Jeffrey and how he kept asking her questions about Hound—nothing made Batty feel shyer than questions—but also because of the leave-me-alone-or-I'll-break-your-arm look on Skye's face. Batty wouldn't have minded either of these things as much if Hound had been there to keep her company, but he would have had to be on a leash, and Hound thought that being on a leash meant playing tug-of-war.

Batty peeked out from behind the bush. Jeffrey and her sisters were leaving. She knew she should follow them, but first she wanted to see what was on the other side of that gate (she had been too far away to hear about the man-goring bull). She crept out from behind the bush and over to the gate and put her eye to a knothole.

What she saw was a field full of clover and daisies, with a barn over on the other side. Now, Batty knew all about horses and their needs. There was a horse farm near the Penderwicks' home in Cameron, where Mr. Penderwick often took Batty to feed carrots to her favorites, Eleanor and Franklin. So she knew a perfect field for horses when she saw one. And while she didn't see any actual horses through the knothole, she figured that didn't mean there weren't any. They were probably hiding just out of her view. Horses could be shy, too.

The gate was locked and too high to climb over. There

was, however, a gap at the bottom big enough to crawl through. Batty carefully wrapped her wings around her shoulders, flopped to the ground, and wriggled under the gate.

Alas, no horses, not even a shy one. Batty looked this way and that, but she was alone on that side of the wall. Oh, well, she would pick daisies instead and take them back to Rosalind to make into a chain. She headed toward the largest clump of daisies and bent to her task.

All was at peace while Batty picked flowers and hummed a song about kangaroos. Above, the birds wheeled cheerfully across the sky. Below, the worms slid happily through the soil. In between, the summer breeze softly ruffled the clover and daisies. But soon the peace was disturbed. Across the field from Batty, the barn door swung open as if shoved by something very strong. And here it came, strong, yes, and big and black. The king of the field, the bull, sauntered out into the sunshine and proudly surveyed his realm.

Skye lagged as far behind Jane and Jeffrey as she could without being too obvious. By the time she finally bothered to catch up with them, Jane was already halfway up the ladder in the stone wall. Jane looked down at her and said, "Isn't Batty with you?"

Skye had forgotten about Batty but wouldn't admit

it for the world. Watching over Batty was always the job of the OAP, or Oldest Available Penderwick, and without Rosalind, Skye was definitely the OAP.

"She was hiding behind a bush when we were at the gate," said Jeffrey.

More showing off, thought Skye, who hadn't noticed Batty behind her bush.

"Maybe I'll be able to spot her from up there," said Jane, then clambered to the top of the ladder and hoisted herself onto the wall. "It's wide enough up here to walk."

"Be careful," said Jeffrey. "It's a long drop."

"I don't see Batty," said Jane, surveying the cottage side of the wall.

"She probably went back to see Hound." Skye hoped it was so. As annoying as Batty could be, losing her altogether wouldn't be so terrific.

"Maybe," said Jane doubtfully.

"I'll go back to look for her," said Jeffrey.

"I'll go with you in a minute. Just let me look for the bull." Jane turned around to look at the field. "Oh, there he is! He must have just come out of the barn."

"Isn't he big?" said Jeffrey.

"Huge!"

So there really was a bull, thought Skye, but she couldn't believe he was as awful as Jane and Jeffrey were saying. It was probably a small bull. Maybe even a fat old cow. She would go up and see for herself, but Jeffrey was in between Skye and the ladder, and she'd stand there all day rather than ask him to move.

"Go on up and look," said Jeffrey, stepping out of Skye's way.

"After you." She wasn't going to fall for his phony politeness.

And then Jane started to scream.

Batty was watching a purple-and-orange bug when Jane screamed. The bug had fallen off a daisy, and Batty had lain down on her stomach to make sure it landed safely. Batty recognized the scream as Jane's, and as Jane had a habit of screaming, more often than Skye, for example, Batty wasn't worried. However, she did look up from the bug.

A bull is so much larger than a bug that at first Batty didn't understand what she was seeing. She looked back down at the bug, who had by now safely scuttled up another daisy stem, then looked back up again, hoping the black monster would be gone. Not only was it still there, it had come a step closer. It was only fifteen feet away.

"Nice horsie," said Batty hopefully.

Now, this bull had never actually gored anyone. It was true that once a tourist had sneaked into the field and dropped his expensive camera in front of the bull, who, quite rightly, stepped on it and smashed it to pieces. But that hadn't been enough of a story for anyone. The first person who told it added a part about the bull scratching the tourist's leg, and the second person who told it turned the scratch into a gouge, and so on, until by the time Cagney repeated the story to Jeffrey, the poor tourist had a gaping stomach wound. When Jeffrey told Jane, he hadn't exaggerated all that much, just changing one doctor to three. Nevertheless, gorer or not, the bull was not sociable, and he particularly didn't like visitors lying in the middle of his favorite daisy patch. It was also possible that he didn't like being called a horsie, because now he shook his horns and stomped his foot at Batty.

Batty knew this was no horse. She suddenly knew lots of things she hadn't known a minute ago, like, she should never have gone under that gate alone, and she should never have disobeyed Rosalind, and she would be a good, dutiful child for the rest of her life if that terrible beast would just stay away from her. For now, she knew she had better just lie very still and wish that Hound were there, and Daddy. Daddy wouldn't let anything hurt her. Oh, Daddy. Oh, Hound. Oh, somebody, please help her.

To Batty's very great relief, a moment later help was on its way, heralded by the noises Jane was making as she ran at Olympian speed along the top of the wall toward the wooden gate. The noises weren't exactly shrieks, or shouts, either; they were more like the sound a fire truck would make if it was trying to speak. It wasn't until Jane reached the gate and skidded to a halt—still on top of the wall—that anything she was saying made sense to Batty.

"BULL! BULL! UP HERE! UP HERE! LEAVE HER ALONE!!!"

The bull swung around toward the wall, and Batty dared to raise her head and look at Jane, who was jumping up and down and waving her arms around like she was directing traffic.

"YEAH, THAT'S RIGHT, YOU MEAN OLD BULL, PICK ON SOMEBODY YOUR OWN SIZE!" screeched Jane.

Then Batty heard what she hoped was more help coming from the other side of the gate, though mostly it sounded like Skye and Jeffrey arguing with each other. A moment later, however, Jeffrey did slide under the gate with Skye right behind him.

"STAY STILL, BATTY, RESCUE IS NIGH!" yelled Jane.

Nervously wondering what *nigh* meant, Batty watched as Jeffrey and Skye raced across the field. They had split apart. Skye was coming toward Batty. Jeffrey was heading straight to the bull.

Jeffrey shouted, "YAH! YAH! COME AT ME, BULL!"

Poor bull. He had simply wanted to quietly munch

daisies in the sunshine, and now his private paradise was full of active and extremely noisy creatures. He hadn't the wits for it. He looked from Jane, to Jeffrey, to Skye, and back to Batty, clearly deciding which to eliminate first. His beady eyes fixed on the one closest to him, the one who had dared pick his daisies. He lowered his head and horns and began a lumbering march to Batty.

Batty saw him coming. She made herself as flat as possible, almost a pancake, then closed her eyes and wondered how much it would hurt. Next thing she knew, she was being lifted like a sack of flour and thrown across someone's shoulder. She opened her eyes. It was Skye! Skye had gotten to her before the bull!

Now Jeffrey was shouting again. "TAKE THAT! AND THAT!" and with each THAT came the sound of a small stone hitting the bull's hindquarters. Jeffrey was drawing the bull's attention to himself so that Skye could get away with Batty. And it was working. The bull was not going to put up with stones being thrown at him, no matter how small. He turned to face this new enemy.

From the wall, Jane screamed, "NOW, SKYE, RUN!"

Carrying Batty, Skye took off at a lopsided run, while the bull pawed the ground and lowered his gigantic head at Jeffrey. CHARGE!

Batty had never had a hero outside her own family.

She had always figured that her father and Rosalind were enough heroes for anyone. But as she bounced crazily up and down on Skye's shoulder during that wild run to safety, a new hero came into her life. She watched Jeffrey work that bull as though trained from birth as a toreador. This way and that he went—darting, weaving, spinning, jumping—always heading away from Skye and Batty. And the bull followed, frantic to rid himself of this exasperating intruder.

Slam! Skye threw Batty to the ground and shoved her under the gate. As Skye started through after her, Jane howled at Jeffrey, "ALL IN FREE, JEFFREY! RUN FOR YOUR LIFE!"

In the field, the final race began. Skye struggled to her feet and planted herself at the gate's knothole. Batty stayed on the ground and peered underneath. Jane kept to her perch on top of the wall. All three watched, terrified, as Jeffrey dashed toward them, the bull only yards behind him.

"OH, HURRY, JEFFREY, RUN, JEFFREY, RUN!" came shrilly from three throats.

Closer. Closer. Closer.

In one swift motion, Jeffrey was on the ground, under the gate, and up again. He and Skye each grabbed one of Batty's arms and lifted her up as Jane leapt off the wall.

"Go!" said Jeffrey, and they all took off just as the

bull crashed his great horns into the gate. The gate shook on its hinges and the bull bellowed with rage, but nobody looked back—they never wanted to see that gate again.

The children were halfway back to the cottage before they felt safe enough to stop. Skye called a halt and everyone collapsed, panting, under a tall pine tree. For a long time there was only silence, as people caught their breath and made sure they had all their arms and legs.

Batty, perhaps unwisely, was the first to speak. "I left my daisies in the field," she said.

Skye raised herself up with murder on her face.

"Don't kill her now, just when we've gone to all that trouble to rescue her," said Jeffrey.

Skye said, "Batty, of all the stupid things you've ever said, that was the stupidest."

"Why did you go into that field, anyway?" said Jane.

"I thought it would be horses," said Batty, checking her wings, which had torn in several places when Skye pushed her under the gate.

"Well, it wasn't horses, you idiot. You almost got us all killed," said Skye.

"We would have been if it wasn't for Jeffrey," said Jane, while Jeffrey blushed and looked at the ground. "Jeffrey, you're a true hero."

"Stop, Jane. It's up to me to thank him. I'm the OAP." Skye sat up and faced Jeffrey, who looked at the ground harder. "I thank you on behalf of the

Penderwick family. Even though I kicked you when you went under the gate before me, and even though I could have taunted the bull just as well as you—"

"Skye!" said Jane.

Skye took a few seconds to concentrate, then went on. "You were brave and intelligent and you saved Batty's life." Here she took a great gulp of air, then rushed on. "I was a jerk before and I apologize, and this is my real apology, because Rosalind and Jane wrote the first one."

Skye stuck out her hand. Jeffrey looked up from the ground and stuck out his hand, too. They shook.

Jane said, "Their hearts laid bare by the near loss of a loved one, the two enemies declared a truce."

"I want to shake his hand, too," said Batty. Jeffrey shook her hand, then Jane's hand for good measure.

A crashing noise from a nearby tree made everyone jump.

"Probably just a squirrel," said Jeffrey.

"Just the same, do you think the bull could break down that gate?" said Jane.

"No," said Skye, but she looked questioningly at Jeffrey.

"No," he said positively.

"Maybe Daddy should go make sure it's safe," said Batty.

"Batty, no! You can't tell Daddy about the bull. You can't even tell Rosalind," said Skye.

"Why not?"

"Because they'll think Jane and I didn't look after you properly."

"You didn't."

"Promise you won't tell," said Jane.

"Can we do Penderwick Family Honor?" asked Batty.

"That's just for the family, Batty, you know that," said Skye, trying to point to Jeffrey without him noticing. Ever since Rosalind and Skye had made up the ceremony after reading a book about a family named Bastable, only Penderwick sisters had done it or seen it done.

"It's okay, I'll leave," said Jeffrey.

"He doesn't have to leave. He saved my life," said Batty. "He's an honory Penderwick."

"Honorary," corrected Jane.

"What do you think?" Skye asked Jane.

"What would Rosalind think?" Jane asked Skye.

"Since it was a question of life and death, I think she'd agree," said Skye slowly. "All right, Jeffrey, you can stay and watch us do it, but you've got to promise you won't tell anybody, even Cagney."

"Okay," said Jeffrey.

"No, no, you've got to swear solemnly," said Jane.

"I solemnly swear not to tell anyone about what you're about to do."

"That's good enough," said Skye, making her hand into a fist and holding it out. "We, the three younger Penderwick sisters, will never tell Daddy or Rosalind about Batty and the bull. We'll come up with a good story about how Batty's wings got torn, and although it will not be the strict truth, it will not be an evil lie, because Batty has learned her lesson and will never go into the bull's field again. Right, Batty?"

"Right," said Batty.

"Okay, I'm done," said Skye.

Jane put her fist on top of Skye's, and Batty put hers on top of Jane's.

"This I swear, by the Penderwick Family Honor!"

Suddenly there came another crashing noise from nearby, and the children knew it was much too loud to be a squirrel. Once again Batty was thrown onto someone's shoulder—this time, Jeffrey's—and everyone took off running. Within seconds, the pine tree was deserted.

So there was no one to see the large, black, terrifying—well, not terrifying—dog when he arrived a moment later. Mr. Penderwick had been wrong about the latch on Hound's gate. It wasn't dog-proof, or at least not Hound-proof, and when the bull was chasing Batty, Hound had sensed her danger with his own peculiar brand of ESP and busted out of his pen.

But where was Batty now? Hound sniffed around the pine tree, puzzled. She had just been here. He lifted his nose to the air and—aha!—caught the scent. Relieved, and faithful through and through, Hound trotted away after Batty.

CHAPTER SIX
Rabbits and a Long Ladder

AFTER BREAKFAST THE NEXT MORNING, Batty took Hound out to his pen to tell him about her adventure with the bull. As he had already heard the story four times the night before, he ignored her and tried to undo the latch on his gate again. But Mr. Penderwick had fixed that after his escape the day before. Hound was trapped.

Batty had just reached the part where Jeffrey yelled YAH! YAH! when Jeffrey himself arrived.

"Hey, Batty," he said. "You swore not to tell anybody what happened."

Batty ran over to the gate and unlatched it to let Jeffrey inside. Jeffrey took a piece of cold sausage out of his pocket and gave it to Hound.

"Hound doesn't count," said Batty. "I tell him everything."

"What did Skye say to your father and Rosalind about your wings?"

"That I got stuck in some prickers, and she and you and Jane had to get me out, and my wings tore. Rosalind fixed them for me."

Jeffrey inspected the neat patches and darns in the filmy fabric. "She did a good job."

"She always does. She takes care of me because Mommy died when I was a tiny baby."

"Do you miss her?"

"No, because I can't remember. Rosalind misses her. She cries in her sleep sometimes. Don't tell anybody I told you that," said Batty. "Now you have to tell me a secret."

Jeffrey leaned down and whispered in her ear, "I was really scared of that bull yesterday. You don't tell anybody, either."

"Okay," said Batty, and they shook hands.

Rosalind came out of the cottage and over to the pen. "Good morning, Jeffrey. Thanks for helping get Batty out of the prickers yesterday."

"You're welcome," he said, looking sideways at Batty, who gave a happy little jump.

"Cagney has invited Batty and me over to meet his rabbits this morning," said Rosalind.

"And he said too many people would scare the bunnies, so Skye and Jane aren't allowed to go, ha ha," said Batty.

"That's enough, Batty. Come on, time to go."

"Sit and say good-bye, Hound," said Batty in her best imitation of Skye being bossy. Hound rolled over on his back. "Hound! You heard me!"

He barked and waved his legs in the air, until Rosalind opened the gate and tugged Batty out of the pen. "Good-bye, Jeffrey. We've got to leave. We don't want to be late for Cagney," she said, heading toward Arundel Hall with Batty in tow.

Earlier that morning, Cagney had arrived at the cottage to water the rosebush. At the same moment, Rosalind had needed to go outside and fill Hound's food bowl. Or so she pretended. What she had really needed was to apologize for the brouhaha of the day before. Almost burning down buildings and saying nasty things was not the picture Rosalind wanted people to have of the Penderwick family. But Cagney had just laughed and said all that had been nothing and when he was nine, not only had he and his brother set their uncle's truck on fire with a firecracker, they had tried to blame it on their sister. And Rosalind had thought that Cagney was very generous to try to make her feel better and wondered why she had never before realized how much she liked baseball caps on boys. Then Batty had come outside looking for Rosalind, and Cagney asked if she wanted to meet the rabbits, and Batty managed to stay visible long enough to say yes. So meet me at ten o'clock at my apartment, said Cagney.

His apartment! Rosalind had never been in a teenage boy's apartment. As she hurried Batty along, she wondered what it would look like. Anna, who had two brothers in college, said that all boys were slobs, that it was in their genetic makeup, but Rosalind wasn't so sure. It was hard to imagine her father, for example, making the messes Anna's brothers did—potato chips in underwear drawers and pizza crusts in beds!—even when he was young.

Rosalind and Batty arrived at the carriage house exactly on time and found the screen door Cagney had described, with a BEWARE OF ATTACK RABBITS! sign nailed alongside.

"Here we are," said Rosalind to Batty, but Batty had vanished. Rosalind found her around the corner, hiding behind a big barrel full of geraniums.

"I've changed my mind," said Batty.

"Oh, sweetheart, Cagney's not a scary boy," said Rosalind.

"Yes, he is."

"But he's already told the rabbits about you. Think how sad they'll be if they don't meet you."

"Tell them I'll come another day."

"They're waiting for you now."

Batty knew how it felt to be disappointed, like

70

when Skye had promised to play Peter Pan with her, then forgotten. She crept out from behind the barrel and walked back to the screen door with Rosalind. Rosalind knocked on the door.

"Come on in! Shut the screen door tight behind you!" came Cagney's voice.

Inside, Rosalind was interested—and relieved—to find a clean and cozy living room with a tidy little kitchen off to the side. She stored up details for her next letter to Anna: a green plaid couch, a pile of books about the Civil War, a half-dozen baseball caps hanging in a row, a framed photograph of Cagney playing basketball.

Cagney stepped out of the kitchen carrying a bunch of fresh parsley. If he was disturbed by the wings that seemed to sprout from the back of Rosalind's legs, he didn't show it.

"Yaz and Carla are under the couch," he said. "Yaz'll come out for parsley, but don't be disappointed if Carla stays under there. She's very shy."

Rosalind heard a tiny "Oh!" behind her. She reached around and took Batty's hand, and together they lay down on the floor and stared under the couch.

Cagney stretched out next to Rosalind and pushed the parsley toward the couch. "Can you see them?" he asked. "Yaz is the brown one with spots, and Carla is that chubby white blob behind him."

At first Rosalind could see only vague shapes, but as

her eyes adjusted to the dark, she saw four glittering eyes and four ears swiveling in her direction. Just as Cagney had said, Yaz soon crawled out, stretched—and yawned!—then grabbed a large piece of parsley and solemnly chewed it to bits. As he started on another, Cagney touched Rosalind's arm and pointed. Fat little Carla was scrabbling out from her hiding place.

"She's not going to let Yaz eat all the parsley without her," said Cagney.

But Carla, for once, wasn't interested in parsley. Something in her tiny rabbit brain had recognized the presence of a kindred spirit in the room. Toward Batty she headed. One hop, two hops, and Carla was nuzzling Batty's hand with her soft nose. This was too much for Yaz. Parsley was one thing, but attention was quite another. In another second, he was snuffling at Batty's other hand.

"What do I do?" whispered Batty, so excited her wings were quivering.

"They want you to pet them, Batty," said Cagney. "It's a great honor. I've never seen Carla go right to a stranger before."

Batty gently stroked the rabbits, Yaz on her left and Carla on her right. "Oh, Rosalind, they love me."

Rosalind and Cagney smiled at each other.

"Thank you," said Rosalind.

"Anytime," said Cagney.

* * *

When Rosalind and Batty left to visit the rabbits, Jeffrey went in search of Skye and Jane. He found them sitting on the front porch of the cottage. Between them was a very flat soccer ball.

"Look what Hound did!" said Jane. "How am I supposed to practice with a punctured ball?"

"Jane's our team's center forward," said Skye. "She's so good that the middle school coach is already coming to games to watch her."

"Don't exaggerate," said Jane, but didn't really mean it. Soccer was the only thing at which she outshone Skye—other than writing books—and she loved it when Skye was generous enough to brag about it.

Jeffrey said, "You can borrow my ball. I'll go back home and get it now if you want."

Jane jumped down from the porch. "Can we go with you?"

"Sure."

But Skye hung back. "What about—I mean—"

"You're worried about Mother," said Jeffrey.

"No. It's not like I'm scared of her. I was just wondering if maybe she'd mind us being there."

"Of course not. Why should she?" said Jeffrey, and started to walk away. Then he looked back over his shoulder at Skye. "Besides, she's not home. She's at a Garden Club committee meeting. Come on."

Jeffrey took Skye and Jane into Arundel Hall through the carved oak door at the front. They found themselves in a magnificent entranceway, so big the whole cottage could have been put into it and there still would have been room for Hound to run around the outside. The wood floors gleamed, as did the wide staircase that rose in front of them. Stained-glass windows on either side of the oak door tinted the sunlight a hundred different colors. Giant blue-and-white vases filled with fresh flowers stood in every corner.

"The splendor of a hundred civilizations," said Jane.

"Don't touch anything," said Skye.

"Let's go to my room," said Jeffrey, heading for the stairs.

But Jane had to see at least one of the rooms that opened off the entranceway. She tiptoed over to the wide doorway on the left. Yet more grandeur. Antique wooden tables with intricately carved legs. Hand-woven tapestries with scenes of unicorns and ladies in tall, pointed hats. Delicate alabaster statues of birds and exquisite oil paintings of gardens. As she told Rosalind later, it was like a museum, except with no velvet ropes or uniformed guards.

Skye dragged Jane away, and the two followed Jeffrey up the staircase, circling around and around, up to the third floor and Jeffrey's bedroom, which was, thankfully, a regular room, not like a museum at all.

There were normal old rugs on the floor, ones you wouldn't be afraid to walk on in your shoes, and the furniture was plain and looked like you could bump into it without scratching it. There was, however, one very special thing that neither sister had ever before seen in a bedroom.

"A piano!" said Skye.

"It's just an upright," said Jeffrey apologetically. "The big one's downstairs."

"Can you play it?" Jane asked.

Jeffrey pulled a soccer ball out from under the bed, twirled it on his finger like a basketball star (he had learned that from Cagney), then headed it to Skye, who neatly caught it.

"Yeah, but not now. Let's go back outside."

"Aren't you any good?" asked Skye sympathetically. She understood all about that. Her father had been forced to cancel her clarinet lessons after the neighbors complained about the practicing.

"It's not that."

"Please," said Jane.

"Well, just a little bit, if you really want to hear." Jeffrey lifted the piano lid and sat down on the stool. Skye and Jane put on their polite faces in preparation to hear awful playing, but what they heard instead was so beautiful that Skye thought Jeffrey was teasing them by playing a recording under the piano (but she checked and he wasn't).

75

Jeffrey broke off after just one minute and grabbed the soccer ball from Skye. "Okay, let's go."

"WAIT!" shrieked Jane. "I want to hear more!"

"Why did you pretend you weren't any good?" said Skye.

Jeffrey's face glowed. "Do you really like it? That was Tchaikovsky, and I've only been practicing it for a while, and of course there should be a full orchestra, too. Music is what I really want to do. My music teacher at school says I'll be able to get into Juilliard, and then, if I'm good enough, I want to conduct someday. But Mother—"

"JEFFREY!"

Everyone froze and looked at each other. Skye recognized the voice. Jane could guess.

"She must have gotten home early," said Jeffrey. He stuck his head out the door and yelled, "I'M IN MY ROOM."

"COME DOWNSTAIRS, DEAR! I BROUGHT THE ROBINETTES HOME WITH ME."

"Mrs. Robinette and her son, Teddy. Mother will expect me to entertain him," said Jeffrey miserably. "You two better stay up here until I can ditch him and come back to sneak you out of the house."

"Why can't we just come with you?" asked Skye.

"You don't want to meet Teddy. His idea of humor is flushing other kids' homework down the school toilet. I'll try to be quick. Maybe I can drown him in the lily pond." Jeffrey slipped out the door.

"Well!" said Skye. She didn't like being stuck indoors because of a bully.

Jane wasn't thinking about bullies. She was standing at one of Jeffrey's windows, gazing out, just as he had on the day the Penderwicks first arrived. And just as Arthur would in her book, poor Arthur, longing desperately for a kind word from someone, from anyone. How would Sabrina Starr first appear to Arthur, way up here at his high window? Jane hadn't decided yet. Could Sabrina pilot a blimp? No, blimps were too big and would get stuck in the trees. A helicopter would be impressive, but also noisy. Sabrina wouldn't want Ms. Horriferous—that was what Jane had named Arthur's evil kidnapper—to hear her coming. But what about a hot-air balloon? Yes! Sabrina could rescue Arthur in a hot-air balloon!

"Jane. Jane!" said Skye. "EARTH TO JANE!"

"What?"

Skye was at another window. "Come here and look. We can climb out and down that big tree."

"Jeffrey said to wait for him."

"It could take him hours to get rid of that Teddy jerk. Help me open this."

Together they pushed the heavy old window up as far as it would go and removed the screen. They tossed the soccer ball out the window, then Skye climbed up onto the windowsill, hopped out and onto a thick branch, and looked down. She wasn't afraid of heights, but it was three long stories to the ground. She grabbed another branch for support and peered around for Jane.

"Where are you?" she whispered.

"I'm writing a note for Jeffrey," said Jane from inside the room. "How about: Flew away, see you later?"

"I don't care what you write. Just hurry up."

A minute later, Jane was next to her on the branch. Carefully they edged over to the trunk, then shinnied down to the next branch, and then another, and then another, until they came to the lowest branch. They were still fifteen feet from the ground.

"Now what?" asked Jane.

"I don't know," said Skye.

"We could go back up."

"Give me time. I'll think of something."

Skye could have thought all day without getting them down from that tree. It was lucky for them that Batty's visit to the rabbits had ended five minutes earlier, which meant that Batty and Rosalind were on their way back to the cottage to tell Hound all about it. But more important, it also meant that Cagney was back at work in the gardens. Jane spotted him pushing his wheelbarrow toward a bed of dahlias about twenty feet from the tree.

"Hi, Cagney," she called.

Cagney turned around in a circle, trying to locate the source of the voice.

"Up here," said Jane.

Then he looked up and laughed. "What are you two doing?"

"We're sort of stuck," said Skye.

"Hold on." He disappeared. Moments later, he was back with a long ladder, which he leaned against the tree trunk. Skye, then Jane, clambered down safely.

"You have our undying gratitude for rescuing us from a fate worse than death," said Jane.

"And could you tell Jeffrey we escaped?" said Skye. "And that he should come over to the cottage for soccer practice when he gets rid of that Teddy Robinette kid?"

"Actually, Cagney, you might be able to help Jeffrey with Teddy," said Jane.

"Jeffrey's trying to drown him," said Skye.

"I'll take care of it," said Cagney, and Skye and Jane slipped away with the soccer ball.

CHAPTER SEVEN
Borrowed Finery

WHEN JEFFREY DIDN'T RETURN to the cottage that afternoon, Jane worked herself into a frenzy imagining that he had gone ahead and drowned Teddy Robinette and that even as she and Skye were happily playing soccer, Jeffrey was being thrown into a dank and dismal cell. Skye told Jane she was an idiot, but she had her own worries. She feared that Mrs. Tifton had discovered the sisters' visit to his bedroom and forbidden Jeffrey to ever see them again.

So it was a great relief for both of them when Jeffrey arrived at the cottage the next morning. The sisters were still cleaning up from breakfast. Rosalind washed, Skye dried, Jane put away the plates and glasses, and Batty stood on a stool and sorted the silverware into the proper slots in the drawer.

"What happened?" said Jane. "Did you kill him?"

"Did your mother kill you?" said Skye.

"Neither. Teddy tripped over a rake and cut his leg and made such a big fuss about it that Mother made me stay inside with him all afternoon and watch television so he could keep his stupid leg elevated. But he won't be coming back. I told him that if he ever did, I'd tell his mother about how he cheated on all his math tests last year," said Jeffrey. "Oh, and Cagney's going to hang a rope ladder from that branch where you two got stuck, one you can roll up when you're not using it so nobody'll notice it from the ground."

"Great," said Skye. "Now we'll always have an easy escape."

"And Jeffrey will be able to escape that way, too," said Jane.

"Why would I have to?"

"Oh, you never know."

"*Dry* the glasses, Skye," said Rosalind. "Don't just hand them to Jane."

Skye rolled her eyes. "Drying is a waste of time when we're going to use everything again at lunch."

"Anyway, Churchie's invited all of you over for gingerbread. Mother is out again, in case anyone cares."

"What's this about gingerbread?" Mr. Penderwick had come into the kitchen to inspect Batty's silverware drawer. It was her great pride to sort everything correctly.

"Churchie makes great gingerbread, and she wants

81

everyone to come eat it. You too, Mr. Penderwick, if you want," said Jeffrey.

"Perfect again, Batty," said Mr. Penderwick, and lifted her down from the stool. "Thank you, Jeffrey, but Cagney's already asked me to inspect the peonies he's hybridizing."

"May we go, Daddy?" asked Jane.

"They're not driving you crazy yet, Jeffrey?" asked Mr. Penderwick.

"Oh, no, sir. Well, except for Skye." Jeffrey nimbly evaded the punch Skye aimed at his arm.

"All right, then. *Vade in pace, filiae.*"

"That's Latin," said Jane.

"I know," said Jeffrey.

Churchie was just taking the gingerbread out of the oven when the five children arrived. It smelled so delicious that everyone immediately forgot they had eaten breakfast.

"There you all are!" said Churchie. "Let me look at you. Here's my old friend, Jane, and this must be Rosalind. And Skye. But didn't Batty come along?"

Rosalind pulled Batty out from behind the door.

"Oh, my! Each prettier than the next," said Churchie.

There was a knock at the door and Churchie let in Harry the Tomato Man. Today his shirt was red, but just like his green one, it had HARRY'S TOMATOES embroidered across the pocket.

"More tomatoes," he said, and set a large cardboard box on the counter.

"Thanks, Harry," said Churchie. "I see you showed up just in time for gingerbread again. Girls, meet the man with the most sensitive nose in Massachusetts."

"Don't listen to her. She'd die of mortification if people didn't show up on gingerbread day," said Harry. "Well, Jeffrey, I hear you've got a wild new bunch of friends here. Cagney's been telling me all about girls sneaking through hedges and hiding in urns and getting stuck in trees. And Farmer Vangelder down the road saw some kids messing around with his bull the other day, but they ran away before he could yell at them."

"Oh, that wasn't us with the bull!" said Rosalind, while Jeffrey tried not to laugh.

Harry glanced over at Skye, who managed to look as though she'd never messed around with a bull in her life. "Well, maybe not," he said. "But you Penderwicks are sure livening the old place up."

"And a good thing, too," said Churchie, cutting huge blocks of gingerbread and putting them onto plates. "Now sit, everyone, and eat."

The Penderwicks peered around, a little overwhelmed, for the kitchen was very large and grand, a kitchen fit for kings, as Jane said later. Besides the normal oven in which Churchie had made the gingerbread, there were two others as big as ovens in restaurants. And there were four refrigerators, three

83

stainless-steel sinks, two long butcher-block tables, and what seemed like miles of counter space. Where should they sit in such a place? But then Jeffrey led them to a sunny nook—as cozy as Churchie herself—where there was a small table with a checkered tablecloth and benches on each side. Everyone piled in, and Churchie served not only gingerbread but whipped cream and strawberries to go on top.

The Penderwicks had never had gingerbread so scrumptious, and even Jeffrey and Harry, who had been treated to Churchie's special recipe many times, went through two pieces each in a flash.

"This is delicious, Churchie, thank you," said Rosalind, wiping whipped cream off Batty's face and shirt.

"Thank you, dear. And wait until you taste the birthday cake I'm planning for next week," said Churchie.

"Who for?" asked Skye.

"Why, Jeffrey, of course. He's turning eleven. Jeffrey, haven't you invited the girls to your birthday dinner?" asked Churchie.

Jeffrey choked on his third piece of gingerbread. It wasn't until Skye pounded him on the back that he could talk at all.

"They don't want to come," he sputtered. "It'll be in the formal dining room, with candles and lace napkins and antique china, and old Dexter will be there."

"What Jeffrey means to say is that Mrs. Tifton's

gentleman friend, Mr. Dupree, will be at the party," said Churchie.

"You mean her boyfriend?" said Skye.

"Mrs. Tifton has a boyfriend?" said Jane.

"That's unbeliev—" said Skye.

"Your party doesn't sound so bad," Rosalind interrupted. "Lace napkins aren't the end of the world. If you want us, we'll come."

"They'd have to wear fancy dresses," said Harry slyly.

"Mother would definitely expect you to be all dressed up."

"Dressed up!" Skye was indignant. "That's ridiculous. It's summer."

"Besides, we didn't bring any dresses with us," said Rosalind. "And we can't ask Daddy to buy us all new clothes for one party."

"You can't come, then. Too bad," said Jeffrey happily.

"Hold on a minute. I have an idea," said Churchie. "Finish up the gingerbread, everyone, then Harry can get back to his tomatoes. The rest of us are going up into the attic."

If the downstairs of Arundel Hall was like a museum, the attic was like a treasure chest. Everywhere the girls looked, they saw the most wonderful things, until they looked somewhere else and saw something even more wonderful. Stacks and stacks, in row after row—

carpets, mirrors, brass and silver trays, painted screens, bookcases stuffed full of books, dolls of all shapes and sizes, bureaus, toy soldiers, cradles, walking sticks and umbrellas, sleds, painters' easels, vases, train sets, old cameras, brocade curtains, and much, much more, so much that you could get lost in there and never care about finding the way out.

While the sisters were still oohing and aahing, Churchie said, "Come, Rosalind, you and I have work to do. Jeffrey, show the others around."

Churchie led Rosalind down an aisle with bureaus on one side and plump couches on the other, then turned left and kept going between marble garden ornaments and tall piles of magazines. One more turn at the lamps with stained-glass shades, and they reached a wide-open area full of clothing, hundreds and hundreds of dresses, suits, shirts, gowns, coats, all hanging in long rows. Rosalind had never seen so many clothes in one place, not even in the Boston department stores.

"Mrs. Tifton has kept just about every piece of clothing she's ever worn," said Churchie. "And every piece her mother, Mrs. Framley, ever wore. And way in the back is a section of her grandmother's clothes."

"They're all so beautiful," said Rosalind, wandering past a rainbow of summer dresses.

"Go over two more rows and look at Mrs. Framley's evening gowns."

Rosalind found the gowns, dozens of them from

long ago, taffeta and lace and satin and velvet, luxury beyond measure. "Oh, my! What did she wear them all for?"

"The Framleys used to give the most fabulous parties. It was long before I came here—I was hired after Jeffrey was born—but Harry's lived in this neighborhood his whole life, and he told me about it. He would help park the cars when the society people came up from New York City. Then there'd be breakfast for thirty on the terrace and formal dinners in the evenings, with live music and dancing after. That was all when Mrs. Tifton was still just a girl. She was the only child, you know, and came late, long after her parents had given up hope for a baby. They worshiped her, brought her up like a little duchess." Churchie had been talking to Rosalind from several rows away. But now she appeared from behind the coats, carrying a striped dress. She held it up to Rosalind. "Yes, this shade of coral is perfect for you. I'll just take it in a little here and there and shorten it to bring it up to date."

"I can't wear one of Mrs. Tifton's dresses," Rosalind protested.

"Why not? I already told Mrs. Tifton we were inviting you, and she'll never recognize the dresses. Who could remember all these?"

"But, Churchie, even if that's true, we can't ask you to do all the sewing, and I don't know how."

"Don't think twice about that. I haven't had a

chance to sew for girls since my daughter was small, and now she's married and living in Boston and keeps having boys. This'll be great fun for me. Here, hold this while I look for something for your sisters."

Rosalind carried the dress over to a big mirror leaning against the wall and looked shyly at her reflection. She had never worn such an elegant, grown-up dress. And it *was* the right color for her. She memorized the details for Anna—soft linen, high waist, sleeveless, round collar, and, Rosalind's favorite part, cloth-covered buttons all the way down the back.

"Churchie, where are you?" she called out.

"Follow the blouses."

Rosalind walked past the blouses, then stopped suddenly at the sight of a gorgeous white dress hanging all by itself at the end of a row. Through its plastic covering she could see yards of satin and tulle sewn all over with tiny pearls. "Oh, is this Mrs. Tifton's wedding gown?"

"Not hers, her mother's," said Churchie, poking her head around a row of silk nightgowns. "I doubt Mrs. Tifton had a fancy wedding gown, and even if she did, she'd never have kept it. That marriage was a Big Mistake and lasted less than a year."

"What happened?"

"Well, you have to go back a little. Mrs. Framley died when young Brenda—Mrs. Tifton, that is—was only seventeen, and the General went into deep mourning. He stopped talking to anyone, even his daughter. The visitors from New York stopped coming, the parties stopped, everything stopped. It was no life for a teenager. As soon as Brenda could, she escaped by enrolling in a small college in Boston. She met a young man there and they were secretly married before she was twenty years old. I guess it was her way of rebelling against her father. He was strict, the old General."

"Where is Mr. Tifton now?"

"His name wasn't Tifton. The General didn't want Brenda to keep her married name after the divorce, and Brenda—she was just as stubborn as he was—refused to go back to being called Framley. She didn't want people to wonder whether or not she'd been married, because, remember, she was very young, and she was pregnant. So they compromised on Tifton, which was the General's mother's last name. I don't know Jeffrey's father's real name, and I certainly don't know where he is. I don't think Jeffrey himself knows any of that either."

"Poor Jeffrey."

"Yes." Churchie plucked a red dress off a hanger and vigorously shook out some imaginary wrinkles, as though by doing so she could straighten up Jeffrey's life. "Anyway, Jeffrey's father left before he was born.

Some say Brenda got tired of him and threw him out, and some say the General paid him to go away because he wasn't good enough to marry a Framley. I do know that Brenda came home to Arundel to have Jeffrey and stayed on here with her father. The baby—Jeffrey—brought the General back to life. He adored the boy, called him the son he'd never had. And then he died, too, when Jeffrey was only seven."

Churchie hung up the red dress and pulled out another, this one cornflower blue. "For Skye, do you think? It matches her eyes."

"Lovely. But, Churchie, this is all so sad."

"It *is* sad. I'll tell you what, though. Jeffrey's been happier since you Penderwicks arrived than I've seen him for a long time."

"Really?"

"Yes, really."

There was a sudden disturbance in the blouses, and Jeffrey, Skye, and Jane appeared, carrying large wooden bows and quivers of arrows.

"Really what?" said Skye.

"Really, you're going to poke somebody's eye out with those arrows," said Churchie.

"We've already decided we'll ask Cagney to cover the tips with rubber to make them safe," Jeffrey explained.

"Humph," said Churchie.

"Rosalind, you should see the stuff over on the

other side of the attic," said Skye. "There's a canoe, and a whole cricket set, and three horse saddles."

"And swords, Rosalind!" said Jane. She plucked an arrow from her quiver and waved it around like a saber. "Ill-bred cur, prepare to meet thy doom on the sword of Sabrina Starr."

"Those are Jeffrey's grandfather's army swords," said Churchie. "Nobody cut any fingers off, I hope."

"There was only one little accident. Skye, show her your hand," said Jeffrey.

Skye held up a hand with two fingers folded under.

"Very nice." Churchie wasn't impressed. "Try not to get blood all over everything."

Jane had tired of instruments of destruction and was noticing the clothes all around her. "Look at all these," she said.

"Churchie is lending us dresses to wear to Jeffrey's birthday party," said Rosalind.

"Wow," said Jane, her eyes huge. "What about the one you're holding, Churchie?"

"I thought it would look nice on Skye."

"Since it's so dainty and ladylike," said Jeffrey.

Now, of course, Skye refused to wear the blue dress. It was only after a long debate, with Jeffrey continuing to cause trouble with his sly compliments, that she finally agreed to wear a dress at all and only then because Churchie found a slim black one that reminded Skye of a dress her mother used to wear. Then Churchie and Rosalind started on Jane, who wanted something both flowingly romantic and thrillingly dashing, two characteristics almost impossible to find in one dress. But Churchie did manage it, discovering way back in the corner a full-skirted navy-and-white taffeta sailor's dress. Jane loved it.

"Now stand still, everyone," said Churchie, and measured the sisters with her cloth tape. "Good. By taking in seams and adding tucks, I can make these dresses look like they were designed for you three. And I think I've found a few long skirts with enough fabric for a sundress for Batty. Where is she?"

Jeffrey found Batty in the middle of a set of wooden animals, all sorts of animals. There was an elephant as big as Batty herself and a mouse as small as her littlest finger. She had taken possession of a rabbit and was hopping it across the attic floor.

"Churchie's going to make you a dress," he said.

"I don't want a dress. I want this rabbit. His name is Yaz."

"You can have the rabbit if you let Churchie measure you for a dress."

"Okay," said Batty, and let him take her back to the others.

Another half hour and it was all settled. Not only would the Penderwicks be going to the formal birthday party that Mrs. Tifton was organizing, they would be wearing her own clothes to the event. That included even her shoes, for Churchie had solved the problem of suitable footwear by unlocking trunks full of shoes of all colors and shapes and telling the girls to choose what they liked. Only Batty's feet were too small to fit into anything, and it was agreed that she could get by with her everyday sandals.

"After all," said Skye. "What does it matter what she's got on her feet when she's wearing those dumb wings?"

"They're not dumb," said Batty, clutching her new rabbit.

"Come on, everybody," said Jeffrey. "Let's go outside and play soccer."

That evening Rosalind called a MOPS to tell her sisters the sad story of Jeffrey's missing father. They were dismayed and wished they could do something, but not even Sabrina Starr had any ideas. They did, however, come up with two helpful resolutions: Do not ask Jeffrey questions about his father, and Get Jeffrey really good birthday presents. Then the sisters went off to their separate rooms, and as each fell asleep, she thought that if there could be anything worse than having a parent die, it would be having a parent who never bothered to meet you.

CHAPTER EIGHT
The Birthday Dinner

Is THERE SUCH A THING AS A PERFECT WEEK? A perfect day, maybe, but seven whole days of paradise? The Penderwicks would say yes, that the seven days between their visit to the Arundel attic and Jeffrey's birthday party would be forever locked in their memories as perfect. Skye liked to say later that the week seemed that way only because they had not yet met Mrs. Tifton. Maybe she was right. Certainly, through either good luck (Skye's theory) or magic (Jane's), Mrs. Tifton did stay out of sight all the way up until the birthday party, leaving Arundel and its treasures to the children.

During those wondrous days, Jeffrey took the girls over every inch of the estate grounds, showing them the old springhouse buried in the side of a hill, the path behind the cottage that led to a bubbling stream, the hiding place under the Greek pavilion, the lily pond with its dozens of frogs, the ancient trash-burying ground where you could dig up old pots and pans, and, on one especially hot day, the controls that turned on the garden fountains. Everyone, even Rosalind, who should have known better, jumped into the streams of water that leapt into the air before Cagney came running to turn the fountains off again, but since it was Cagney, he just laughed and told them not to do it again.

On top of all that, each sister had her private joys. For Batty, it was Hound sleeping with her every night and, almost as special, daily visits with Rosalind to see Cagney's rabbits. Sometimes Cagney was there, but more often he wasn't, and then Rosalind would let Batty open the screen door just far enough to slide in two carrots, then watch from outside as Yaz and Carla nibbled. For Jane, it was soccer practice every day with Skye and Jeffrey, plus the Sabrina Starr book, which was growing ever more exciting. (Sabrina had made several flying visits to Arthur but had not yet figured out how to get him out of his window and into her balloon.) For Skye, the best times were the long, wild romps through the gardens with Jeffrey by day and the calm of her clean, white, tidy bedroom at night. And Rosalind? She cherished Cagney's early-morning visits to water the Fimbriata rosebush and the time he'd take afterward to sit and talk on the porch. By using Anna's First Rule of Conversation with a Boy—Ask lots of questions—Rosalind was learning a lot about Cagney. Like how he was saving his money to go to college, because he wanted be a high school history teacher and baseball coach. And when he had accomplished all that, he would buy a house in the country and raise a family with enough kids for a basketball team (a baseball team being too large even for him) and, in his spare time, write books about the Civil War. Every night, Rosalind carefully wrote down everything Cagney had said and sent it in a letter to Anna.

And so the days slid by, each better than the one before, and everyone thought that their perfect vacation at Arundel would last forever and ever and ever.

Then came the birthday party.

"Smile, troops!" said Mr. Penderwick, and pushed the button on his camera. Nothing happened.

"The other button, Daddy," said Rosalind.

"Ah, yes." He peered over his glasses at the camera. This time there was a flash of light.

"Take another one, Daddy. Hound wasn't smiling," said Batty.

"He doesn't deserve to smile," said Skye. A half hour earlier, Hound had thrown up on Skye's—that is, Mrs. Tifton's—silver party shoes. Rosalind had thoroughly cleaned the shoes, but now they squished at each step.

"Do my knees show in the picture?" Jane asked. Her knees were scraped from the morning's soccer practice.

"I told you before, your skirt is long enough to cover the messy parts," said Rosalind.

"Okay, here we go," said Mr. Penderwick. Another flash of light went off.

"Daddy, no! Batty had her gum side toward the camera," said Rosalind. Batty had gotten chewing gum stuck in her hair that morning, and though Rosalind had cut it out as neatly as she could, there was now an awkward gap in Batty's curls.

"Okay, one last shot. *Vincit qui patitur*," said Mr. Penderwick.

"Concentrate, everyone," said Rosalind.

"Beautiful," said Mr. Penderwick as the camera flashed again. "My four princesses."

Rosalind looked anxiously at her sisters. They did look nice. Skye was as sleek and undainty in her black dress as she could possibly be, and Jane was so delighted with her sailor's dress that she kept twirling the full skirt out like a parachute. Batty was, of course, wearing her wings, but Churchie had chosen a bright yellow fabric for her, saying that if the child insisted on being a bug, you might as well let her be a brightly colored bug. And Rosalind hoped that she herself looked all right. Her striped dress fit like a glove, and she had piled her hair on top of her head. She had put on lipstick, too, but then rubbed it off before coming downstairs. Anna believed that lipstick looked silly until at least eighth grade.

"Are we ready to go?" she said. "Who has Jeffrey's presents?"

"I do," said Jane, picking up a large shopping bag.

"Everyone say the rules again," said Rosalind.

"Please and thank you to everything, keep your napkin on your lap, and don't argue with or make faces at Mrs. Tifton," said Jane and Batty.

"Skye?" said Rosalind.

"I know the rules," said Skye.

"Hound wants to come with us," said Batty, and Hound barked to back her up. "He says he'll escape if we don't take him." Hound's latest attempts at jail-breaking had been to dig under the fence. He hadn't made it out yet, but Mr. Penderwick was spending a lot of time filling in holes.

"Don't worry about Hound," said Mr. Penderwick. "He and I are going for a long walk in search of *Rudbeckia laciniata*."

"And you won't miss us for dinner, Daddy?" said Jane.

"I'll be fine. Hound and I are having hot dogs. You

all enjoy yourselves and say happy birthday to Jeffrey for me."

The girls took the long way to Arundel Hall, as Rosalind didn't trust they could make it through the hedge tunnel without damaging their finery. Once in the gardens, they made a quick detour to hide the shopping bag under the Greek pavilion—they had agreed earlier to give Jeffrey his presents after the party, without Mrs. Tifton around—then walked around the mansion to the kitchen door. They wanted to show Churchie the results of her handiwork.

"Churchie, it's us," said Rosalind, knocking.

But it was Cagney who opened the door. "Wow, you girls look great."

"Except for my shoes." Skye shifted from one foot to the other to demonstrate her squishiness. "It's Hound's fault they're wet."

"Okay. Except for Skye's shoes, you girls look great." He grinned at Rosalind, who blushed and wished she hadn't.

"Cagney, bring them in here," called Churchie from the kitchen.

The girls went into the kitchen, where they found not only Churchie, tossing a big salad, but Harry, leaning against the sink and eating a dinner roll. Today his shirt was yellow.

"I came over for the fashion show," said Harry.

"Don't listen to him," said Churchie. "He and Cagney came to eat. Now let me look at you girls."

They formed a line. Jane curtsied, then twirled her skirt around.

"You all look gorgeous, just like flowers in bloom."

"Thanks to you, Churchie," said Rosalind. "We love our dresses."

"Don't they look gorgeous, Harry?"

"Absolutely." Harry picked up another dinner roll.

"Where's Jeffrey?" asked Skye.

"In the dining room with Mrs. Tifton and Mr. Dupree," said Churchie.

"The boyfriend," whispered Jane to Skye.

"Yes, the boyfriend. Mrs. Tifton told me to escort you there when you arrived."

"Oh, dear." Rosalind straightened Jane's sailor collar and smoothed Batty's curls over the gum place.

"You'll do fine," said Cagney. He gave Rosalind a thumbs-up sign, which she ignored with all her might, determined not to blush again.

"After all, what can she do to us?" said Skye. "Let's go see Jeffrey."

Churchie led the girls through the pantry and down a short hallway and stopped beside a wide doorway. "Here we are. Now get in there and do yourselves proud." She gave them each a kiss on the cheek, then disappeared back toward the kitchen.

Jane peeked around the edge of the doorway and

100

whispered, "They're standing at the other end of a very, very long room."

Rosalind took a firm grip on Batty's hand—she knew poor Batty would rather be anywhere else—and stepped into the entranceway. For once, Jane hadn't been exaggerating. The dining room was so long that the people standing together at the other end looked like little dolls. The backs of little dolls, anyway, for all three were facing away from the girls. Rosalind hesitated. It didn't seem right to creep down that long room behind Mrs. Tifton's back.

"Let's shout hello," said Skye.

"That would not make a good first impression," said Rosalind.

"Sabrina Starr and her companions were too proud to sneak up on their enemies," said Jane.

"Let's go home," said Batty.

"What are we, men or mice?" Skye stood tall, her shoulders back, to show that she, at least, was no mouse.

"You're right," said Rosalind. "Troops, advance."

They struck out, Rosalind in front with Batty, Skye and Jane behind. One step, two steps, onward they went, and still the people at the other end didn't turn. Eight steps, nine steps, ten steps, down that long, long quiet room. Or it would have been quiet if not for Skye's shoes. It seemed that the closer the girls got to Mrs. Tifton, the louder Skye squished, like a monster jellyfish with feet. Rosalind looked pleadingly at Skye, but Skye shook her head and frowned—she couldn't help it.

The three people at the end of the room were looking larger now. Mrs. Tifton was in a fancy purple dress, and Dexter and Jeffrey were both wearing suits. Jeffrey also seemed to be weighed down by something slung over his shoulder, something thick and brown that hung all the way to the floor.

"What's Jeffrey doing with that log?" said Batty.

"I don't think it's a log," said Rosalind.

"It looks like a log," said Batty.

Thirty-four, thirty-five, thirty-six steps.

Then Jeffrey looked over his shoulder. For one brief second, Rosalind saw a look of misery on his face, and then it was gone, and he was smiling. Slowly and carefully, he turned himself and the big brown thing around. Whatever it was, it was heavy, and now it was hidden behind him and even more mysterious.

"Mother, the Penderwicks are here," the girls heard him say.

Mrs. Tifton turned to face them.

And the sisters immediately wished she would turn away again. Walking down that long room behind her back was nothing to doing it under her gaze. Oh, what a gaze! The girls tried to describe it to their father later. It was like steel, said Rosalind. No, like a hawk, said Skye. You could tell she doesn't like animals, said

Batty. She was just like the Queen of Narnia, not Queen Susan or Queen Lucy, but the mean one that turned everything into winter, said Jane. Not that she isn't pretty, added Rosalind. Pretty, humph, said Skye, she looked like her face would crack if she laughed.

Altogether, Mrs. Tifton was one of the last people you would want to talk to, let alone eat dinner with, and if it wasn't for Jeffrey, Rosalind would have turned her sisters around and marched them right back out of the room. But they couldn't desert Jeffrey, not like that, not on his birthday.

So they kept on walking. Forty-nine steps, fifty, fifty-one, fifty-two, and finally fifty-three.

"Halt," said Rosalind under her breath, and they all did.

"Ah," said Mrs. Tifton, then paused for a moment—which seemed like an hour to everyone else—while she inspected the Penderwicks. "So these are the girls my son spends all his time with. What do you think, Dexter?" She turned to the man standing beside her.

Dexter was handsome—the girls agreed on that later—dark-haired, with just a touch of gray at the temples and a distinguished-looking mustache. But unfortunately, he looked like he knew exactly how handsome he was.

"Very nice," he said. Then he smirked. Rosalind

had seen smirks before, but never one quite so—smirkish. Again she thought of flight—however cowardly and craven—but then glanced at Jeffrey and saw that the look of misery was back. She gave him a thumbs-up, just like the one Cagney had given her, and was rewarded by a smile.

"Now, Jeffrey, introduce us," said Mrs. Tifton.

"This is Rosalind," said Jeffrey. "She's the oldest."

"Hello, Rosalind," said Mrs. Tifton. "What a charming dress."

Rosalind froze. What was she supposed to do now? With everything else to worry about, she had forgotten to worry about Mrs. Tifton recognizing her own dresses.

"You got it at the Salvation Army. Right, Rosy?" said Skye.

"Yes, that's right," said Rosalind, and while she was grateful to Skye for rescuing her, she thought the Salvation Army was going a little too far.

Mrs. Tifton seemed to think so, too. "Oh," she said, looking even stiffer than before.

"These are Skye, Jane, and Batty," said Jeffrey quickly.

"And this is Mr. Dupree." Mrs. Tifton laid her hand possessively on Dexter's arm. "Now, Jeffrey, why don't you show the Penderwicks your birthday present?"

"All right," said Jeffrey without enthusiasm, and heaved himself around again, dragging his burden back into view. It wasn't a log. It was a large leather golf bag.

"Put it down, Jeffrey, and show us the clubs," said Mrs. Tifton.

Jeffrey slid his shoulder out of the bag strap and stepped away from it. It wobbled a moment, about to fall, but Jeffrey caught the shoulder strap just in time. He pulled a club halfway out. "This is a driver. You hit the balls with it."

"I didn't know you liked golf, Jeffrey," said Skye.

"Well . . . ," said Jeffrey.

"It's a beautiful golf bag," Rosalind offered.

"A golf bag fit for kings," said Jane.

"Mr. Dupree is an excellent golfer. He's arranged for Jeffrey to have lessons at the country club," said Mrs. Tifton.

"A country club fit for kings," said Jane.

"Only kings who belong," Dexter touched his mustache complacently. "It's private, you know."

"A *private* country club fit—" Jane stopped short when Skye lightly jabbed her in the ribs. Rosalind hoped Mrs. Tifton hadn't seen the jab, but she agreed that it had been necessary. Jane was plainly slipping into her nervously-spouting-nonsense mood.

"Now, Jeffrey, why don't you seat your guests?" said Mrs. Tifton.

Jeffrey let go of the shoulder strap and turned away. Once again the bag started to wobble, and though Skye attempted a flying save, she was too late. The bag crashed to the ground, narrowly missing Mrs. Tifton's high heels.

"Jeffrey, for heaven's sake, be careful!" she said. "Those clubs cost me the moon."

"Sorry, Mother," he said, struggling to haul the thing back upright. He lugged it across the room and leaned it in the corner.

"Well!" said Mrs. Tifton. "Now maybe we can sit down. Dexter, pour me a glass of wine."

The table wasn't as long as the room, but still it was much too long for the number of people eating dinner—the seven place settings of china and lace napkins were all stuck mournfully at one end, leaving the rest of the vast, shiny surface empty. The head of the table was for Mrs. Tifton, and she indicated that Jeffrey would be on her right and Dexter on her left. Jeffrey led Rosalind to the chair next to Dexter's, and Batty, who was still holding Rosalind's hand, went along and sat down beside her. That left Skye and Jane to fight it out for the seat next to Jeffrey, but they solved that by agreeing that Skye could have it for dinner and Jane for dessert.

Rosalind wasn't happy to be so close to the smirking Dexter, but she didn't want any of her sisters near him, either. To avoid him, she turned toward Batty, just in time to see a pair of butterfly wings disappearing beneath the table. She grabbed them before they vanished altogether and quietly hauled Batty back up into her chair.

"Stay in your seat," she whispered.

"I don't like it up here," said Batty.

"I don't, either. Stay in your seat, anyway."

Rosalind looked across the table at her other sisters. Skye was talking to Jeffrey and tapping a spoon against her crystal water glass—please don't let her break it, Rosalind prayed—and Jane was staring fixedly at the ceiling. What was she looking at? Glancing upward, Rosalind was startled to see that the ceiling was painted all over with men and women in togas, lolling around and eating grapes.

"That cost a fortune," said Dexter.

Rosalind jumped. "Excuse me?"

"The ceiling. Some French artist had to lie on his back on scaffolding to paint it, just like Michelangelo in the Sistern Chapel. Set Mrs. Tifton's great-grandfather back thousands."

Rosalind had learned in art class about Michelangelo painting a ceiling somewhere, though Sistern Chapel didn't sound quite right. But she knew it was impolite to correct a grown-up, even an obviously unintelligent one, so she decided to ignore both Dexter and the toga wearers above her. Instead, she looked around at the paintings on the walls of the dining room. Most were of people, and from their air of self-satisfaction, Rosalind guessed they were relatives of Mrs. Tifton. Particularly that stern-looking man hanging behind Skye. He was wearing an olive green uniform all covered with medals and looked like he ate nails for breakfast.

"Rosalind, that's my dear papa, General Framley," said Mrs. Tifton. "Now, who do you think looks exactly like him?"

"You?" said Rosalind, wishing people would just leave her alone.

"Me?" Mrs. Tifton gave out a little tinkle of a laugh. "Of course not. I meant Jeffrey. He's the image of his grandfather."

Skye snorted, and Jane looked doubtfully from the portrait to Jeffrey and back again. Rosalind held her breath, for she knew that either one was capable of blurting out that Mrs. Tifton might want to get her eyes checked. But peace was maintained, for just then Churchie sailed into the room, pushing a silver cart on wheels.

"Dinner is served," she called out gaily.

For the next few minutes, Rosalind could relax. There was lots of bustling around and serving of delicious food, and Churchie talked the whole time about how hungry everyone must be and how beautiful everyone looked and how it wasn't every day people turned eleven and how everyone should be careful not to get food on her wings, this last said along with a gentle pinch of Batty's cheek. But then Churchie was gone, and Rosalind started to worry again. She knew that the odds were low of getting through the whole meal without some sort of upset. If only no one would talk, then they might be safe.

As if she had read Rosalind's mind and disagreed, Mrs. Tifton started up a conversation. "Girls, I must apologize for the lack of male escorts. We had hoped that Jeffrey's friend Teddy Robinette would be here, too, but he got a bad cold at the last minute."

"Jeffrey's told us all about Teddy," said Skye. "Haven't you, Jeffrey?"

"Mm-mmh," said Jeffrey, busying himself with his napkin.

"A nice boy from a good family," said Mrs. Tifton. "And now, you must tell me all about yourselves. I like to know everything I can about Jeffrey's friends. Let's start with Skye." She looked at Jane.

"I'm Jane," said Jane.

"Excuse me," said Mrs. Tifton. "Well, there are a lot of you, aren't there."

"I play soccer," said Jane, glancing over at Rosalind, who nodded encouragingly. "And I write books. I'm writing one right now about—"

"How interesting," interrupted Mrs. Tifton. "And Mr. Dupree here is in the publishing business. Maybe he can give you some pointers."

"Really?" asked Jane.

"Sure, kid," said Dexter. "Bring your book around when you've finished it."

"Wow! I will! Thanks!" said Jane, all aglow. Rosalind's

heart sank. She hated it when untrustworthy people made promises they wouldn't keep.

"Now, what about you, Rosalind?" said Mrs. Tifton.

"I'll bet she wants to be a fashion model," said Dexter, showing all his teeth.

"Fashion model!" said Skye.

And that was it for Skye's self-control. Rosalind knew it, and she barely cared anymore. Still, she tried to stop her sister. "It doesn't matter," she said.

"It does matter," said Skye. "None of us will do anything as idiotic as fashion modeling."

Looking daggers at Skye, Mrs. Tifton tossed off her glass of wine, then poured herself another. "And, pray tell, what *will* you do?"

Skye was undaunted. "I'm going to be a mathematician or maybe an astrophysicist. Jane's going to be a writer, of course, and Rosalind hasn't decided yet, but Daddy says that she's well suited for international diplomacy."

"And I suppose your littlest sister is going to be president of the United States," said Mrs. Tifton.

Everyone looked at Batty, who was trying to hide behind the water pitcher.

"She wants to be a veterinarian," said Jane. "But Daddy thinks she's going to be a Renaissance woman."

"That means someone who's good at a lot of different things," Skye explained.

"Mr. Dupree and I know what it means, Jane," said Mrs. Tifton.

"I'm Skye."

"Blue Skye, blue eyes," said Jane. "That's how you can remember. You see, the rest of us have brown eyes."

Mrs. Tifton looked at Jane as though Jane had purple eyes with yellow stripes, then said, "Well, Dexter, we may not know much about astrophysics, but at least we know what Jeffrey's going to be when he grows up."

"So do we. A musi—ouch!" said Skye. Jeffrey had kicked her under the table.

"Papa and I planned it out long ago, when Jeffrey was still a baby. He'll attend Pencey Military Academy and then West Point, just like Papa did, and he'll be a soldier, just like Papa was. And someday, Jeffrey, too, will be a brave and beloved general." Mrs. Tifton turned around in her chair and raised her glass to the portrait of General Framley. "Cheers, Papa. We miss you."

CHAPTER NINE
Shocking News

"**I** TRIED TO STOP YOU FROM COMING to the party, but you wouldn't listen to me. I knew it would be awful," said Jeffrey. He and the four sisters were outside on the wide stone veranda that ran along Arundel Hall. They had escaped as soon as they could, which meant not until they had finished dinner and birthday cake. Not that anyone had much of an appetite left after Mrs. Tifton's announcement, not with that grim old General staring down at them like a horrible warning— Someday Jeffrey Will Be Just Like Me.

"It wasn't that awful a party," said Jane.

"Yes, it was," said Skye. "Jeffrey's right."

"Shh! They'll hear you." Rosalind was peeking through big French doors back into the dining room.

Mrs. Tifton and Dexter were still at the table, drinking coffee.

"I don't care if they hear us," said Jeffrey. "That was the worst birthday party ever in the history of the world. You shouldn't have been here. It was humiliating."

"It was partly our fault, though," said Rosalind. "We upset your mother."

"Jane and her country club fit for kings," said Skye.

"What about you and your astrophysics?" said Jane.

"Actually, I liked that part," said Jeffrey, his frown disappearing.

"You never told us about that Pencey Military Academy," said Jane.

"I don't like talking about it." Jeffrey's frown was back. "Besides, Grandfather didn't start there until he was twelve, so Mother says I can wait until I'm twelve, too. Anything can happen in a year. Mother could forget all about it, right?"

"Sure." Jane didn't look sure.

"Have you told her you don't want to go?" Rosalind asked.

"Whenever I try, she starts talking about how wonderful my grandfather was and how much I remind her of him. Do I seem like the military type to you?"

"No," said Skye firmly.

"Not that you couldn't be a ferocious hero and all that," said Jane.

"Thanks, but I'd hate going to war." Jeffrey flung himself onto a stone bench. "And golf! I hate golf, too. I can't believe Mother bought me those stupid golf clubs. And now I have to be tortured with lessons at the country club. Why not just kill me now and be done with it."

Batty sat down next to Jeffrey. "Don't be upset. We have more presents for you."

While Jane ran off to retrieve the presents from under the Greek pavilion, Rosalind tried to cheer up Jeffrey with the story of Hound throwing up on Skye's shoes. Skye and Batty helped by acting it out, with Batty as Hound and Skye as herself, squishing dramatically up and down the terrace. They had him almost forgetting about Pencey and the golf clubs—for a moment, they thought he was even going to laugh—when Jane arrived.

"Here they are, wrapped and everything." Jane dropped the bulging shopping bag at Jeffrey's feet.

"But no birthday card," said Rosalind.

"We had one, but Hound ate it," said Batty.

The first present was a book from Rosalind and Jane—and Mr. Penderwick, too, because they'd run out of pocket money, Jane told Jeffrey—about famous orchestra conductors, with lots of photographs of them and their orchestras. Jeffrey thought this a wonderful gift. *Much* better than golf clubs, he said. The second present was Skye's—a brown-and-green camouflage

114

hat identical to hers. Jeffrey put it on and looked happier than he had all evening.

The third present was from Batty, and only Rosalind knew what it was. Jeffrey held it up to his ear and shook it, but it made no sound.

"What is it?" he asked.

"Open it," said Batty, wriggling with excitement.

"Animal, vegetable, or mineral?" he asked.

"OPEN IT!" shrieked Batty, almost tumbling off the bench.

It was a framed photograph of Hound.

"Oh, thank you." Jeffrey gave Batty a big smile. "I love it."

"But, Batty," said Jane. "That's your favorite picture of Hound, the one you keep by your bed."

"She said she wanted to give it to Jeffrey. I asked her four times. Right, Batty?" said Rosalind.

"Yes. And maybe he'll let me borrow it back sometime," said Batty.

"Batty! You can't say that!" said Rosalind, and Jeffrey grabbed Batty and tickled her until she shrieked. Jane looked like she was about to join in when Skye held up her hand and told them all to be quiet.

"I hear music."

Everyone listened. The music seemed to be coming out of another set of French doors, farther down the veranda.

"That's the drawing room," said Jeffrey. "Let's go look."

The five of them crept along the veranda and peered into the drawing room. By now, it was almost dark outside, so that while people inside wouldn't be able to see the children, the children could easily see them.

It was Mrs. Tifton and Dexter, and they were dancing.

"It's a waltz," whispered Jeffrey.

"How do you know?" whispered Skye.

"Mother made me take dance classes last year. Here, I'll show you." Jeffrey grabbed Skye. "ONE, two, three. ONE, two, three." He moved forward to the music and ran smack into her. "You're supposed to go backward when I go forward. It's called following."

"Forget it," said Skye. "Show Rosalind."

Jeffrey took hold of Rosalind and tried again. "ONE, two, three. ONE, two, three." This time it worked, and they waltzed along the veranda.

Jane clutched Batty and pushed her backward. "ONE, two, three. ONE, two, three. We're doing it," she whispered excitedly, and, forgetting to watch where she was going, shoved Batty into a giant pot of flowers. They both crashed to the ground, giggling.

In a flash, Skye ran over from the French doors and shoved Jane and Batty off the veranda. "Hide!" she hissed at Rosalind and Jeffrey. In seconds, all five of them had leapt off the veranda and crouched behind a thick clump of bushes. They heard Mrs. Tifton and Dexter step onto the veranda.

"There's no one out here, Brenda," said Dexter.

"I thought I heard something," said Mrs. Tifton.

"Probably just Jeffrey running around with his girl-friends."

Skye silently pretended to gag and throw up, which would have made Jeffrey laugh if Rosalind hadn't clapped her hand over his mouth.

"Don't even say such a thing. He's much too young for girlfriends," said Mrs. Tifton. "And when the time comes, he will pick a girl from a background similar to his own. Not like those Penderwick girls, who are a little vulgar, don't you think? Definitely not in our class."

"No one's in your class, darling."

"Flatterer." The girls could almost *hear* Mrs. Tifton preening like a peacock. "Truly, though, Dex, I'm concerned about the Penderwicks' influence on Jeffrey. He hasn't been himself since they arrived."

"You worry too much. In a few weeks, they'll be gone and forgotten. Come on, let's dance out here," said Dexter, and for a while all the children could hear was Mrs. Tifton's high heels on the veranda. One, two, three. One, two, three.

There was no pretend throwing up or smothered laughter in the bushes now. It was hard to know which of the five children was the most uncomfortable.

Jeffrey appeared to be the worst—he was purple with embarrassment—but the Penderwick family pride had been greatly wounded. Skye looked ready for battle, and Rosalind was furiously scolding herself. She knew that hearing bad things about yourself is one of the punishments for eavesdropping. Her father had taught her that a long time ago. Her wonderful father. How he would despise what that woman had just said. Class is as class does, he would say, but probably in Latin.

Dexter was talking again. "Just think, Brenda, this could be Paris. Close your eyes and imagine waltzing along the Seine."

"Mmm, Paris," said Mrs. Tifton, like she had just eaten chocolate mint ice cream. "I haven't been to Paris for years, not since Papa took me there for my sixteenth birthday. I haven't been anywhere for years."

"We wouldn't have to stop at Paris. We could go to Copenhagen, London, Rome, Vienna, anywhere you want. Let's set a date."

"We've been over this already."

"I need to go over it again. How much longer do I have to wait? You know I want to marry you, Brenda, and take you on a fabulous honeymoon."

"And you know I want to marry you."

Jeffrey gasped, so loudly that Rosalind thought his mother and Dexter had to hear it. But they were too absorbed in each other.

"Then what are we waiting for? Explain it to me, love."

"Jeffrey—"

"This is about us, not Jeffrey."

"If I just knew what would be best for him."

"What's best for his mother is best for him, and I know what's best for his mother."

Then came some noises that sounded suspiciously like kissing. Rosalind put her hands over Batty's ears and glanced at Jeffrey. He had his face buried in his arms. How much more could he take?

The music stopped and Dexter was talking again. "I've been looking into Pencey. Do you know they allow boys to start as young as eleven? Why not send Jeffrey there this year?"

"You mean this September? Next month? Dexter, he's my baby."

"Of course he is, but the sooner he starts Pencey, the better chance he'll have of eventually going to West Point. You've told me how much that meant to your father."

"It meant the world to him." Mrs. Tifton's voice dropped. "Since he didn't have a son to follow in his footsteps."

"Well, I know someone who's glad the General had a daughter."

The dreadful kissing noises started up again and

lasted for what seemed like an eternity. When Mrs. Tifton and Dexter at long last broke apart and went back inside, no one wanted to talk or even look at each other. Finally Rosalind touched Jeffrey on his shoulder.

"It'll be all right," she said.

Jeffrey shook her hand away and stood up. "I've got to go."

"See you tomorrow?" asked Skye.

"I guess so." Jeffrey angrily rubbed his eyes with the back of his hand. "Thanks for coming."

"Happy birthday, Jeffrey," said Jane.

"Don't forget your presents," said Batty.

But he was already gone. The sisters crept sadly back onto the veranda to gather up the gifts.

"We're lucky Mrs. Tifton didn't notice all this stuff." Rosalind picked up the torn wrapping paper and crumpled it into a ball.

"She was too busy kissing that Dexter." Skye kicked the stone bench.

"Rosalind, was Jeffrey right?" asked Batty. "Was this the worst birthday party ever in the history of the world?"

"Of course not," said Rosalind.

Skye kicked the bench again. "Close, though."

Late that night, in her attic bedroom, Jane finished another chapter of her book. In this one, Ms. Horriferous told Arthur that she meant to keep him locked up forever.

"Why? Why?" he cried.

"I like to torment you," she cackled.

"Please, please, let me go," begged Arthur.

"Never!" she cried, and swept out of the room.

Arthur furiously beat his fists against the walls of his prison. He would do anything to get away. Where was Sabrina Starr? When would she return for him? And would she have figured out how to get him out the window and into her hot-air balloon?

Jane put down her pen and closed her notebook. She knew she should go to bed, but she wasn't at all sleepy. She kept going over the evening in her mind, especially the very end, when Jeffrey ran off alone into the darkness. What a horrible way to find out that your mother was getting married. And that the man she was marrying wanted to ship you off to military school a whole year early!

Jane needed someone to talk to. She slid her feet into slippers, tiptoed downstairs, and pushed open Skye's door. "Skye, are you asleep?"

"Yes."

"I have to talk about Jeffrey."

"Go away or I'll kill you."

Jane shut the door, went back down the hall, and pushed open Rosalind's door. Although all her lights were out, Rosalind wasn't in bed. She was standing at the window, staring out into the night.

"Rosalind?"

121

Rosalind turned. "Oh, Jane, you startled me."

"What were you doing?"

"I was thinking about—um, lots of things. Why are you still awake?"

Jane sat down on Rosalind's bed. "I can't stop worrying about Jeffrey."

"We talked about all this on the way home. There's nothing we can do right now."

"We could ask Daddy to adopt him."

Rosalind sat down beside her. "Don't be ridiculous."

"We could write a letter to Mrs. Tifton explaining why Jeffrey shouldn't go to military school."

"We'd do better with the adoption scheme," said Rosalind. "Go to bed, Jane. It's late."

"You're right." Jane stood up, then sat down again. "I have something else to talk about."

Rosalind sighed and lay down. "Go ahead."

"Do you think it would be disloyal to Jeffrey if I asked Dexter for help with my book? He's a real live publisher. I might never meet another one. This could be my last chance."

"The point isn't whether or not you'd be disloyal to Jeffrey. The point is whether Dexter meant what he said about helping you, and he probably didn't, because he's not a nice person. This is not your last chance. You're only ten. So forget all about it and go back to sleep."

Jane slipped back upstairs and got into bed. She

told herself that Rosalind was right, that it was silly to count on anything from a creep like Dexter. But then Jane had an idea and sat up in bed with excitement. Maybe Dexter wasn't always a creep. Maybe he had two sides, like that Dr. Jekyll person in the play the sixth grade had put on last spring. Dr. Jekyll was a nice man until he drank a secret potion, which turned him into the horrible Mr. Hyde (played to dastardly perfection by Rosalind's friend Tommy Geiger in a fake black beard). Maybe the man who was Mrs. Tifton's nasty boyfriend was the bad, Mr. Hyde side of Dexter. Then the good, Dr. Jekyll side of Dexter called Mr. Dupree!—could be a wise, kind publisher, who would be only too eager to help young writers find their destinies. It was that man, the Mr. Dupree side, who had said at dinner he'd look at the Sabrina Starr book when it was finished.

Jane settled back onto her pillow. It was a theory, maybe a good one, maybe not. But she would keep it to herself, because her sisters would only laugh at her. In the meantime, she would work hard and write the best book she could. She closed her eyes and went to sleep, and all that night, she dreamt about being a famous and distinguished author.

CHAPTER TEN
A Bold Escape

THE DAY AFTER HIS BIRTHDAY PARTY, Jeffrey showed up at the cottage ready for soccer practice as though nothing had changed from the day before. But something *had* changed, and everyone knew it. Now Jeffrey had the double threat of Dexter and Pencey hanging over his head, without knowing which was going to happen or when. It didn't make it any easier that the Penderwicks' time at Arundel was more than half gone. In a week and a few days, they would be heading back to Cameron. Without knowing Jeffrey's fate? Maybe never to see him again? It was unthinkable.

Then, too, there was the problem of Mrs. Tifton all of a sudden being everywhere. It was the upcoming Garden Club competition, Jeffrey said. His mother was obsessed with Arundel winning first prize and so was spending all of her time outside, fussing over details and driving Cagney nuts. And driving the children nuts, too. If they were kicking soccer balls at the marble thunderbolt man—he made a good goaltender—Mrs. Tifton showed up to scold. If they were taking bets on how high the lily pond frogs could jump, she said they were bothering the frogs. If they were cooling off in the shade of a rose arbor, she told them—well, anything, it seemed, just to keep them moving along.

It was bad for everyone, but it was hardest on Batty. For while the three older Penderwicks loathed Mrs. Tifton, Batty feared her. As she told Hound when they were alone at night, Mrs. Tifton was the meanest person she had ever met. So mean, said Batty, that the flowers died when she walked by, which wasn't true, but Hound knew just what she meant. And so Batty did everything she could to avoid Mrs. Tifton and generally succeeded by hiding behind a bush or a sister. But there was one occasion when Mrs. Tifton caught Batty all by herself, and the consequences were dreadful.

It all started one morning a few days after the birthday party.

"Please, Rosalind," said Batty. She was clutching two fat carrots.

"I already told you, Batty. I'll take you to see the rabbits later, but not now." Rosalind was simultaneously baking brownies and reading a book about Civil

War generals. Cagney had lent her the book, and she wanted to be able to say something intelligent about Ulysses S. Grant and Appomattox the next time she saw him.

Batty cared nothing for Grant and Appomattox. "Cagney says the bunnies expect me in the mornings now. By later, they'll already think I've bandoned them."

"Abandoned."

"They'll think I've *a*bandoned them."

"I'm right in the middle of making these brownies, and then I have to finish my letter to Anna so Daddy can mail it for me when he goes into town," said Rosalind. "So it's either later or not at all. You've seen the rabbits every morning for a week and a half now. You can skip one day."

"No, I can't."

"Honey, I'm sorry. Why don't you ask Jane or Skye to go with you?"

" 'Cause they'll say no."

"Ask them. If they won't, I promise we'll go later, okay?"

Batty carried her carrots out to the front yard, where Jane and Skye were painting a face on a big round piece of cardboard. The face had a smirk and a big mustache, and in case that wasn't enough of a hint, the initials D. D. were painted across the bottom.

"Jane, Rosalind says she can't take me to see Yaz and Carla and will you?"

"Sorry," said Jane. "Cagney figured out how to put rubber tips on those arrows and Jeffrey's bringing them over so we can do target practice. Can't you ask Daddy?"

"He's out collecting plants," said Batty. She looked at Skye with no hope.

"Forget it, midget," said Skye.

Batty gloomily wandered into the backyard and over to Hound's pen, where Hound was sleeping on his back with his legs sticking up in the air. Maybe she should just go by herself. Batty leaned against the fence and pondered the idea. Stay in the yard, that was always the rule. But no one had ever said where the yard for the cottage actually ended. She could ask Rosalind if maybe the yard stretched all the way to where the rabbits lived. Or she could go see the rabbits first and ask Rosalind later. Which? She would ask Hound.

"Hound! Wake up!" said Batty. But he only grumbled and fell over onto his side.

That was a good enough answer for Batty. She looked around to make sure no one was watching, then took off for the hedge. Be quick like a bunny, she said to herself as she popped through Jeffrey's gap and across the gardens—with only a brief detour to the lily pond to visit the frogs—then to the carriage house and Cagney's door. Panting, but triumphant and still unobserved, Batty knocked.

Cagney wasn't home. But that was all right. Often he wasn't, and Batty knew exactly what to do, for he had explained it all to her and Rosalind. Call out to Yaz and Carla, open the door and slide the carrots inside, then you can watch through the screen as they eat the carrots. But never forget the most important part, Cagney had said. You must latch the door securely again, because if you don't, Yaz will shove it open with his nose and run away, and he can't survive outside. A fox would kill him, or a hawk or an eagle. Then Carla would wither away and die of loneliness, because they're best friends and love each other very much.

Batty pressed her face to the screen and peered in. Yaz and Carla were asleep on the rug, side by side, their noses touching. "Wake up," called Batty softly. Carla flipped one ear in her direction, then Yaz did, and a minute later they were both yawning and stretching and doing their wake-up dance—running around in a circle, jumping and changing direction midair, then running around in a circle the other way.

Batty carefully unlatched the screen door and shoved her two carrots inside. Though she knew she shouldn't, she also stuck her nose inside, just in case Yaz wanted to come over and rub noses. This was her downfall. For while her nose was still inside, she heard a familiar and dreaded sound behind her on the brick path that led to Cagney's door. Tap tap tap tap tap tap tap.

Panicked, Batty whirled around to face her enemy and discovered that the situation was even worse than she had thought. For it wasn't just Mrs. Tifton—Dexter was there, too. The carrots were forgotten. The rabbits were forgotten. And Cagney's most important rule about latching the screen door was forgotten.

"Good grief, Dexter, here's one of the Penderwicks," said Mrs. Tifton. "Run along back to the cottage, Bitty or whatever your name is. Your father didn't rent the whole estate, you know."

Batty felt as helpless as a fly in a spiderweb. She would have liked more than anything to run along to the cottage, but getting *past* those two grown-ups was impossible.

"Why doesn't she say anything?" said Mrs. Tifton. "She didn't speak at Jeffrey's party, either. Did you notice that?"

"Maybe something's wrong with her." Dexter tapped the side of his head significantly.

"Or she could be deaf." Mrs. Tifton leaned toward Batty. "CAN YOU HEAR ME?"

Batty didn't mind being thought deaf, but she was annoyed that Dexter didn't think she would understand what his head tapping was all about. She knew that meant crazy, even if she was only four. I'm not crazy, she thought, you mean old silly man. And she concentrated all her attention on wishing Dexter's mustache would turn green or orange or fall off his face and onto the ground right there and then. Which is why she didn't notice that behind her, the screen door was slowly being pushed open. It wasn't until it bonked into Batty's back that finally, too late, she remembered about Yaz and his tendency to escape. Letting out a yell, a kind of garbled combination of Yaz and no—YAZHNO!—she threw herself against the door, relatching it. But Yaz was already through. There was a brush of fur against Batty's ankle, a streak of brown down the path and across the driveway, and he disappeared into the gardens.

The adults had noticed nothing but Batty's cry. Mrs. Tifton straightened up, not pleased. "Yazhno? When she does talk, she doesn't make any sense."

"Like I said." Dexter tapped his head again.

"Maybe you're right. Another reason to be glad her family is leaving soon. Seven days and counting." She put her arm through Dexter's. "Come along. Our Cagney must be somewhere else."

And away they strolled.

Batty was in shock. She had done everything wrong. All of that about the yard stretching to where the rabbits lived and maybe she could go by herself—wrong, wrong, wrong. She had disobeyed Rosalind, she had disobeyed Cagney, and she had annoyed Mrs. Tifton. But worst of all, it wasn't she who was being punished for it. It was Yaz and Carla, who would soon both be dead because of Batty's wickedness. Wicked, wicked Batty. She couldn't go back to Rosalind now. There was only one thing to do. Find Yaz and bring him home.

By the time Rosalind finished her letter to Anna, the brownies were done. She took them out of the oven and let them cool, cut them into squares, and neatly wrapped four of the squares in tinfoil. These were for Cagney. Just the other morning, while watering the Fimbriata rosebush, he'd told Rosalind how much he liked brownies. He said they were just about his favorite food—brownies and the hot dogs you get at Fenway Park. Not that she'd made the brownies for Cagney, she told herself while sticking a cheerful yellow bow onto the tinfoil. As she had written to Anna, she would never sink so low as to try to get a boy's attention with food. Or with Civil War knowledge. Brownies also happened to be her father's favorite snack, and the Civil War truly was fascinating, though she'd never realized it before.

Batty hadn't come back inside since leaving with the carrots. Rosalind figured she'd either convinced Jane to take her to visit Yaz and Carla or she'd started playing and forgotten all about them. Rosalind considered looking for Batty before taking the brownies to Cagney's apartment, just in case she still wanted to go.

But no, Rosalind decided, with only a tiny twinge of guilt. Cagney might be there, and it was more fun to see him without little sisters around.

Though she didn't know it, Rosalind took the same route Batty had earlier, even including the detour to the lily pond. Rosalind loved this pond. She found it peaceful but a little sad, too. For some reason it always made her think of Hamlet's girlfriend, Ophelia, and how she drowned herself when she went insane. Or maybe it was when Hamlet went insane. Rosalind wasn't sure which, and Anna said it was Rosalind who was insane to be reading Shakespeare. But Rosalind's mother had loved his plays and always quoted him. Like: I pray thee, Rosalind, sweet my daughter, be merry. Her mother must have said it to her a thousand times. Lately, Rosalind had been thinking about her mother even more often than usual and wondering whether or not she would like Cagney. Though how anyone could not like Cagney was beyond Rosalind's power of imagination. He's probably perfect, she thought, and, leaning over the edge of the pond, picked a lily and tucked it behind her ear.

She set off again for the carriage house, still not directly, for the sisters had learned the best routes for avoiding Mrs. Tifton. This one took her around the pond, up past the old springhouse, down through the lilac walk, and—

Her luck ran out. She was face to face with Mrs. Tifton and Dexter.

"This is too much, really too much," said Mrs. Tifton. "Penderwicks everywhere, like a swarm of locusts. And who gave you permission to pick one of my lilies?"

Rosalind clapped her hand over the flower, mortified. "No one—I mean, I'm sorry, I shouldn't have."

"That's right, you shouldn't have, like you shouldn't be here in my gardens. I'm getting very tired of running into your family."

"I'm sorry," said Rosalind again. "I was just going to leave Cagney some brownies."

"The way to a man's heart, et cetera, et cetera," said Mrs. Tifton. "Remind me to bake for you sometime, Dexter."

"You already have my heart, darling."

"Yes, well, of course." She patted her hair complacently. "So, Rosalind, you may leave your little offering at the carriage house, but if you're hoping to see Cagney, I sent him out to buy mulch. Then hurry back to your own side of the hedge, and if your youngest sister is still hanging around, take her with you."

"Batty?"

"Bitty, Batty."

"The one with the wings." Dexter made the wings sound extremely ill-bred and tacky.

Rosalind's stomach took a plunge. "You saw Batty at the carriage house?"

"That's what I said, isn't it?" said Mrs. Tifton. "Now run along."

133

Rosalind slid past them, not knowing whether she was more upset by Mrs. Tifton's nasty comments or about Batty being at the carriage house. Had Batty really decided to go see the rabbits all by herself? She knew she wasn't allowed to wander around alone like that. Rosalind dashed toward Cagney's apartment, the lily dropping unheeded from her hair. When she arrived, there was no sign of Batty. But had she been there earlier? Rosalind peered through the screen door. What she saw did not calm her. There were two fat carrots on the rug right inside the door. That wasn't right. Yaz never let carrots lie around uneaten.

"Rabbits," called Rosalind. Nothing. She called again, and this time one nose came poking out from under the couch. It was Carla. She gave Rosalind a long, sad gaze, then pulled back and disappeared.

What had Batty done?

At about the same time that Rosalind was picking the lily, Jane was aiming an arrow at the cardboard target of Dexter's face, now nailed to a tree. She let the arrow fly.

"That's the third time you've missed the whole target. Are you blind?" said Skye.

"Take off your hat, Jane," said Jeffrey.

Jane was wearing a yellow rain hat, because Skye and Jeffrey were wearing their camouflage hats, and she didn't want to be the only one without a hat. But it wasn't the hat that made her miss the target—she could see perfectly. It was lack of concentration. She was too busy trying to figure out how to get bows and arrows into her Sabrina Starr book.

She strung a fourth arrow. Maybe she could use them in the hot air balloon scene. Sabrina could shoot an arrow at Arthur's window with a message tied to it. No, she had already used carrier pigeons to take messages back and forth. Wait—here was an idea! Sabrina could tie one end of a rope to an arrow and the other end to the balloon basket, then shoot the arrow through Arthur's window. Arthur could then use the rope to haul the balloon close enough that he could climb out the window, onto the tree branch, and into the balloon basket. Oh, that was perfect!

She pulled the string of the bow again and shot the arrow. *Thwonk!*

"Bull's-eye!" shouted Jane.

"First strike for Jane," said Jeffrey.

"That wasn't a bull's-eye," said Skye. "You won't disable Dexter with a glancing blow to the cheekbone." She walked over to the target and pointed to a little dent in the cardboard, which was all there was to show for any hit. With their rubber tips, the arrows just bounced off the target and fell harmlessly to the ground.

"That's not mine. My dent should be on the nose," said Jane.

"Not even close," said Skye.

"We need something to put on the arrows so they'll leave a better mark where they hit," said Jeffrey.

"Blood," said Skye.

"Ketchup," said Jeffrey.

"I'll get some ketchup while you take your turns," said Jane, and ran off.

Long before Jane reached the cottage, she heard Hound barking. This wasn't odd in itself—Hound was always barking. But this was his something-is-not-right-in-my-world bark. Although Jane knew that it could mean anything from a leaf had fallen in his water bowl to an elephant had walked into the yard, she hurried to his pen.

Hound bounded over to her, barking even more furiously. Jane could see nothing wrong, however. His water and food bowl were full, he didn't look like he'd been hurt, and his pen looked the same as usual—lots and lots of holes along the fence dug by Hound and filled in by Mr. Penderwick.

"What's wrong, screwy dog?" she said.

"Wow woof woof wow," said Hound, crazily pawing at the gate.

"Lonely, huh? Poor Hound. But you've got to stay here. You wouldn't be good with arrows."

"Woof." Hound disagreed, but it wasn't arrows he was interested in. It was escape. He needed absolutely,

136

positively that very minute to get out of the pen and go help someone.

If Batty had been there, she would have understood. But Batty wasn't, which was part of Hound's distress. And Jane wasn't as proficient as her little sister at dog language. "Sorry, buddy," she said. She hadn't gone half a dozen steps when she heard a big thump and a jubilant bark. She whipped around just in time to see Hound land on the wrong side of the fence and dash away. Hound was on the loose!

It had long ago been proved that Hound could not be caught by one Penderwick sister alone. It took at least two, and three was better, especially if one of them was Batty. Jane needed help. She sprinted back to Jeffrey and Skye, arriving just as Jeffrey was about to shoot another arrow at Dexter. "It's Hound," panted Jane. "He jumped over his fence and ran away."

Jeffrey threw his bow and arrow to the ground. "Mother's been in and out of the gardens all day, fussing about her Garden Club competition. If she sees Hound, she'll go nuts. She still doesn't even know he's living here."

The three took off for the tunnel at top speed, burst through the hedge, and ran smack into Rosalind.

"Yaz is missing. I think Batty let him escape," said Rosalind wildly. "We have to find him before Cagney comes back."

"And Hound's escaped from his pen," said Skye.

There was dead silence as the full horror of the situation struck everyone. Then the three sisters started talking all at once.

"Quiet!" Jeffrey shouted, waving his arms in the air. "Hound could be here any second. Skye, you guard the tunnel and keep him from coming through."

"Right." She slipped back through the tunnel.

"The rest of us will look for Yaz. I'll take from here to the pond," said Jeffrey.

"I'll look in the flower beds along the hedge," said Jane.

"And I'll look between here and the carriage house, in case he's sticking close to home," said Rosalind, desperately hoping that's what a rabbit would do.

Jeffrey and Jane flew off. Rosalind turned and walked slowly back toward the carriage house, stooping to peer under every flower and leaf, around every urn and statue. The sun and shadows played tricks with her eyes—over and again, dashes of white that she hoped were part of Yaz turned out to be flowers or stones. When at last she reached the final flower bed before the driveway, she was so discouraged she almost ignored one last white splatter. But when the splatter twitched in a most un-flower-like way, Rosalind shaded her eyes from the sun, squinted, and breathed a tremendous sigh of relief. For there was Yaz, crouched calmly in a bed of nasturtiums, chomping on a leaf.

"Oh, Yaz, thank goodness you're safe," Rosalind said. "Remember me and all those carrots my little sister and I gave you?"

Yaz stopped chewing and tipped his head to one side. He seemed to be pondering the carrot memory and approving it. Rosalind almost believed he nodded before biting into another leaf. She dropped to her hands and knees and inched her way toward the renegade. Silently and smoothly she went forward, while Yaz cheerfully nibbled away, though always with one bright eye fixed on Rosalind.

Rosalind felt that everything was now all right in the world. She was going to catch Yaz. She was very close now. A tiny bit more, he was just barely out of reach, and then—

A frenzied mixture of barking and shouting broke out behind Rosalind.

"No!" she cried as Yaz stamped out one frenzied thump of DANGER and took off like a shot. Rosalind whipped around to see him zigzagging madly toward the lily pond. She knew only one creature fast enough to overtake the rabbit now, and unfortunately that creature was about to do just that. Hound had obviously gotten past Skye and through the tunnel, for there he was, bolting through the gardens toward Yaz. Skye was tearing along behind him, and Jane and Jeffrey were racing from their different positions, trying to reach Hound before he caught Yaz.

As if all that weren't awful enough, Rosalind heard yet another shout coming from a different direction, accompanied by the sound of high heels stomping on the asphalt driveway.

"WHAT'S THAT DOG DOING IN MY GARDENS?"

Marching toward Rosalind was a very angry Mrs. Tifton. As Rosalind watched, Mrs. Tifton tried to break into a trot, only to stumble, for one of her shoes had just lost a heel. This did not improve her temper.

"Rosalind!" she screeched.

With no time to be polite, Rosalind turned her back on Mrs. Tifton. She knew she was too far away to help Yaz. She could only stand and helplessly watch the wild chase toward the pond. Skye and Jane were far behind now, but Jeffrey was still in the game, running toward Hound in a last heroic attempt to cut him off. He made one magnificent dive in Hound's path, which Hound neatly sidestepped. One, two horrible moments of silence, then Jane's howl of anguish rang out across the gardens. There was only one thing that howl could mean. Rosalind started to cry. She hated to cry, but more, she hated pain and suffering and death, and she hated herself because she was going to have to tell Cagney that Hound had killed Yaz.

Now here came poor, stupid, murderer Hound, galloping toward her with something brown and white in his mouth. Following him in a ragged line were Jeffrey, Skye, and Jane. And Mrs. Tifton was still approaching from the other direction, limping now, and muttering not very polite words. Rosalind wiped the tears from her eyes. She was the OAP. She could handle this. She stood firm and waited.

Hound reached Rosalind with a happy bound and dropped Yaz at her feet. He barked. Aren't I great? Aren't I wonderful? Rosalind looked at him sternly but hadn't the heart to scold. Seconds later, Jeffrey, Skye, and Jane arrived. Jane was sobbing. Skye grabbed hold of Hound's collar and held on like she'd never let go again. Jeffrey, pale but alert, stepped in front of the little furry body on the ground, screening it from sight just as Mrs. Tifton hobbled up to them.

"Whose dog is this? Is this your dog?" Mrs. Tifton looked accusingly at Rosalind.

"Yes, ma'am," said Rosalind.

"I tell you to stay out of my gardens, and instead you bring your huge, disgusting dog over here to tear through my delphiniums? Three days before the Garden Club competition? How dare you! No one even told me you had a dog!"

"I'm sorry. It won't happen again."

"I'm sorry, I'm sorry, that's all you say. But you're

141

right, it won't happen again. I'll be talking to your father about this. And about how all of you girls continually make free with my property." She turned to Jane. "What are *you* crying about, Skye?"

"Nothing," said Jane, tears streaming down her face.

"Humph," said Mrs. Tifton. "Come along back to the house, Jeffrey."

"In a minute."

"Now. Dexter wants to give you some tips on your golf swing."

"I'd like to help get Hound back to the cottage, Mother. It's important. I'll be home as soon as I do that."

His mother stared witheringly at Jeffrey, but he had quite a stare of his own to give back. The Penderwicks didn't know which way it would go, but in the end, it was Mrs. Tifton who dropped her eyes and tromped unevenly away, giving off almost visible fumes of rage.

"We don't want you getting into trouble," said Rosalind to Jeffrey. "You didn't need to disobey."

"Yes, I did. This *is* important." Jeffrey crouched down and gently stroked Yaz. There was no blood, thank heavens.

"Should we bury him?" said Skye.

"We have to wait for Cagney," said Rosalind.

"Cagney!" said Jane, and cried harder.

"We could at least put him in a box or something," said Skye.

Jeffrey picked up the small body and cradled it to his chest. Rosalind, fighting back her tears, touched the darling bunny one last time. He was still warm. If she didn't know better, she'd think he wasn't dead. She could almost feel him breathing.

"OH!" shrieked Rosalind. "LOOK!"

Everyone looked and shrieked, too, for Yaz had opened his eyes. He looked as surprised as they were.

"Is he alive?" cried Jane.

"Is he okay?" cried Skye.

Rosalind and Jeffrey felt Yaz all over and could find nothing wrong.

"Why, Hound didn't kill Yaz," said Jeffrey. "He caught him for us."

Hound barked proudly. Aren't I wonderful? Aren't I great? And everyone who wasn't holding Yaz fell on Hound with cries of praise and delight.

"Jeffrey, take Yaz back to Cagney's apartment," said Rosalind. "Right now before anything else happens. We'll get Hound home and lock him up in the cottage."

But Hound didn't like that idea. When Skye tugged on his collar to get him moving, he tugged in the other direction and started his something-is-not-right barking all over again.

"What's wrong with him now?" said Jane. "He already got to rescue Yaz."

Hound's barking got worse. WOWWOWWOW-WOW.

"What's he upset about?" said Jeffrey. "Can you understand him?"

"Only Batty really—" Rosalind stopped and looked frantically around her. "Batty! Where's Batty?"

CHAPTER ELEVEN
Another Rescue

As soon as Batty had decided she must find Yaz, she tried to do just that. She looked all over the Arundel gardens for him, calling his name, begging him to show himself. Three times she went around all the statues, urns, fountains, and beds full of flowers, but nowhere could she find a rabbit. Despairing, she was sure Yaz was gone for good. Now there was only one thing left for her to do, if only she could be brave enough.

She *was* brave enough, she told herself sternly. And so, at about the same time that Rosalind left the cottage with brownies for Cagney, Batty climbed over the low stone wall that marked the back edge of the Arundel gardens. She was going home. Not to the cottage. To her real home, in Cameron, where there was no

Mrs. Tifton, no lost Yaz, and no Cagney and Carla, whose hearts Batty had broken. She would get there by nightfall and sleep in her own bed, and maybe, just maybe, by the time her sisters and father came home, too, they wouldn't be so very angry at her.

She knew the way. Arundel was in the mountains, and Cameron wasn't, so she must keep going downhill. And wherever the land was flat, she must head toward the sun, for Skye had once said that Cameron was east of Arundel and that east—whatever that was—had something to do with the sun. Unfortunately, soon the sun was overhead and gave no clues whatsoever, but still Batty plodded on.

If she hadn't been so unhappy, the first part of her journey would have been pleasant. It was mostly through fields, and there were bright, waving wild-flowers, big bugs that hopped as high as her nose, and even some butterflies that followed Batty from one field to the next, apparently thinking her a giant Queen of the Butterflies. And just when she was so hot she thought she'd die, she came to a shallow, trick-ling stream, and she waded right in and sat down in the water and thought how nice it was without an OAP to tell her no.

But best of all was what she found in the field next to the stream—two horses standing behind a fence, just waiting for Batty to come along and pick handfuls of clover to hold up high enough so that they could snuffle at it with their velvety black lips. That is, the horses were the best of all until Batty noticed that one was brown with spots like Yaz and the other one was white like Carla and that they nuzzled each other with great affection, and she thought about how sad they would be if one of them ran away and left the other alone forever.

Batty said good-bye to the horses and trudged off.

"She's not here in the gardens," said Rosalind. She, Jeffrey, Skye, and Jane had just met back at the marble thunderbolt man for a status report.

"I checked all around the carriage house and my house and with Churchie. She hasn't seen Batty all day. And Cagney's still not back," said Jeffrey.

"She's not in the cottage. After Skye and I took Hound back, I looked in every room, under the beds, in her secret passage closet, everywhere," said Jane.

"And I searched all over the cottage grounds," said Skye.

Rosalind shaded her eyes from the sun and stared into the distance, first in one direction and then another, hoping desperately for a glimpse of a little girl in wings. But there was nothing except gardens and, farther away, trees and then mountains.

"It's time to tell Daddy." She was very pale.

"He's not back from town yet," said Jane.

"Then what should we do? What can we do? Oh, this

is all my fault! And I promised—I promised Mommy I would take care of her." Rosalind's legs collapsed and she sank to the grass, sobbing. Jane clumsily patted her, but this only seemed to make her cry harder.

"We've got to find Batty," said Skye to Jeffrey and Jane.

"What about Hound?" said Jeffrey.

"What about him?"

"Can he track people?"

The three Penderwicks stared at Jeffrey. Why hadn't they thought of that? A little color came back into Rosalind's face and she leapt to her feet.

"Come on!" she cried, and took off for the cottage with the others tearing after her.

Hound was in the cottage barking like an insane creature. As soon as Rosalind opened the front door, he made a determined dash for freedom, almost knocking down Jane, but Jeffrey tackled him and held on until they could explain to him what had to be done.

"Jane, go get something of Batty's," said Rosalind.

It took only a minute for Jane to fetch Funty from Batty's bedroom. Rosalind stuck the blue elephant under Hound's nose. "Find Batty," she said.

Hound gave her a look of great disdain. He knew his job better than they did.

"I think he understands," said Jeffrey.

"I hope so," said Rosalind. "Let him go. We'll follow him."

In a flash, Hound was out the door and speeding toward the hedge tunnel.

Batty had been walking in the hot sun for over two hours, though she herself didn't know how long it had been—she had no watch and couldn't tell time, anyway. She only knew that she was hungry and thirsty and tired. And now she had come to a road. As roads go, it wasn't a busy one—she had been standing there for a few minutes already, and not one car had gone by—but a road was a road, and her father had forbidden her to ever, ever cross one by herself.

Her spirits were flagging. Cameron now seemed too far away to reach before night came, and she wished all of a sudden that she could turn around and go back to the cottage. But she couldn't go back. She had to go forward, which meant that she had to cross this road. Batty looked left, then right, then left again. There were still no cars. She closed her eyes for courage, put one hesitant foot onto the asphalt, then paused. She had heard something. Could it be? Yes, there it was again. A bark! Batty whirled around and saw the most wonderful dog in the world, flying straight to her.

"Hound!" she cried, and threw her arms open. He leapt right into them, and the two tumbled to the ground and rolled over and over in a frenzy of joyful reunion. But the happiness didn't last, for within seconds Batty heard shouting. She raised her head and saw Jeffrey racing toward her and, behind Jeffrey, her three sisters, all of them frantically yelling. And although Batty couldn't understand a word—for they were still too far away—she knew it had to be about poor Yaz and what a terrible child she was. She jumped up, took hold of Hound's collar, and tried to haul him toward the road. "C'mon! We have to get away!"

Hound dug his four feet into the ground and resisted. There was no way he was letting Batty cross that road. She tugged and he tugged back until, in despair, she let go of his collar. If he wouldn't go with her, she'd just have to keep going alone. Batty closed her eyes again and ran out into the road, just as a car came into view.

"It was amazing, Daddy! Jeffrey snatched her right out of the jaws of death," said Jane.

"You're scaring him," said Skye. "The car wasn't even close."

"I was scared," said Rosalind. "I was terrified." She reached over and took hold of Batty's little arm. She never wanted to let go of it again.

"And Jeffrey gave me a piggyback all the way to the cottage," said Batty, snuggling cozily with Funty in Mr. Penderwick's lap. "Now, Rosalind, tell again how Hound rescued Yaz."

"We've already heard that one four times. We need to put you to bed," said Mr. Penderwick. The family was still gathered around the kitchen table after dinner.

"No, Daddy, not yet," said Batty comfortably.

"A little while longer, then." Mr. Penderwick would have denied his youngest nothing that night. "But I need to talk to your sisters seriously, so no more Yaz stories for a few minutes, okay?"

"Okay," Batty said, and fell instantly asleep with her head on his shoulder.

"Mrs. Tifton called me this afternoon," said Mr. Penderwick.

"Uh-oh," said Skye.

"She was rightly upset about Hound racing around her gardens and I apologized and assured her that it would never happen again. As it will not," he said, looking under the table at Hound, who was finishing off a steak grilled just for him. "But that wasn't the difficult part of the conversation. Mrs. Tifton also let me know in strong language that I don't exercise enough control over you girls."

"Oh!" said Rosalind, offended.

"What did you say?" asked Skye.

"*Satis eloquentiae, sapientiae parum.*" His daughters looked at him with blank faces. "Yes, well, Mrs. Tifton doesn't know Latin any more than you girls do, thank heavens. It wasn't a particularly polite thing to say, especially as she may be right."

"Of course she's not right," said Rosalind.

151

"Look at what happened today," he said. "Could I ever have forgiven myself if we'd lost Batty for good?"

"But we didn't," said Skye.

"Mrs. Tifton doesn't know what she's talking about, Daddy," said Jane. "You're a perfect father."

"Not perfect, Jane-o." Mr. Penderwick shook his head. "There's more. Mrs. Tifton seems to believe that the Penderwicks are a bad influence over Jeffrey. According to her, when she told him to go back to Arundel Hall after the Hound incident, not only did he refuse, but he didn't come home for another hour."

"He was busy finding Batty!" said Skye.

"I know that, and you all know that, but Mrs. Tifton's idea is that Jeffrey is suddenly rebellious and it's because of you girls."

"If Jeffrey is rebelling, which I don't admit for an instant, it's because of awful Dexter, not us," said Skye.

"And Dexter is—?"

"Mrs. Tifton's boyfriend," said Rosalind. "He is— not nice."

"Though not as un-nice as Mrs. Tifton," said Jane.

"Almost," said Skye darkly. "It's a wonder even she can put up with him."

"People sometimes make unexpected choices when they're lonely," said Mr. Penderwick.

"Mrs. Tifton lonely!" Rosalind hadn't thought of that.

"Good grief, don't start getting all sympathetic,"

said Skye. "You can't feel sorry for someone who thinks that we—the Penderwicks!—are a bad influence on Jeffrey."

"We're not, are we, Daddy?" said Jane.

"I see nothing in Jeffrey to make me think he's under any bad influence whatsoever, let alone yours. He's a great boy. And now that he's saved Batty's life—"

"Twice!" said Jane.

Skye frowned horribly at her to shut up, but luckily Hound chose that moment to toss his steak bone into his water bowl, and the resulting flood distracted Rosalind and Mr. Penderwick. When the mess was cleaned up, Mr. Penderwick started again.

"As I was saying, in some cultures it's believed that when a person saves someone from death, he or she forever owns a part of that someone's soul. So Jeffrey is now linked to our family, whether he likes it or not."

"That's kind of romantic," said Jane.

"Romantic, shmomantic. What the heck would Jeffrey do with Batty's soul?" said Skye.

Batty opened her eyes sleepily. "He could marry me," she said.

"Marry you!" Jane and Rosalind laughed while Skye fell off her chair and rolled around the floor like Hound when his back itched.

"Nevertheless," said Mr. Penderwick seriously. His daughters knew that tone. Everyone quieted down and Skye got back into her chair. "We must remember that we're guests here at Arundel. I know that Mrs. Tifton is not the warmest of women, and the one time I met her with Cagney, she tried to impress me with her knowledge of *Campanula persicifolia*—she pronounced it *Campanula perspicolia*—well, that's beside the point. What I'm trying to say is that whatever you think of Mrs. Tifton, you must still be on your best behavior in her home."

"You're right, Daddy," said Rosalind. "We'll be perfect ladies."

"I won't," said Skye. "I will, however, be gentlemanly."

"It's the same thing in the end," said Jane.

"It's not the same thing at all."

"Yes, it is—"

"Enough. *Tacete*." Mr. Penderwick stood up, Batty still in his arms. "Let's all put ourselves to bed. It's been a long day."

CHAPTER TWELVE
Sir Barnaby Patterne

THE THREE OLDER PENDERWICK SISTERS AGREED not to tell Jeffrey about owning Batty's soul and possible marriage. And Batty herself didn't discuss it with Jeffrey. On the other hand, Hound heard a great deal about the wedding and about how he would be dog of honor, but since Hound was good at keeping Batty's secrets, Jeffrey didn't have to be troubled with the information. The boy was under enough strain as it was.

It wasn't just the looming threat of military school and Dexter as a stepfather, or the now obvious disdain Mrs. Tifton had for the Penderwick girls, or even Jeffrey's first golf lesson at the country club, which would have made him hate golf more if he hadn't already hated it with all his heart. It was also the Garden Club competition. Mrs. Tifton had discovered that the judge was going to be that distinguished English gardener, Sir Barnaby Patterne. Mrs. Tifton could not bear to fail in the eyes of a man with Sir in front of his name. No, never, never. And so her obsession with the visit became a frenzy. She was even spotted once in shorts and sneakers, pulling up weeds and muttering to herself.

It was not calming for Jeffrey and the Penderwicks. As much as they could, they stayed on the cottage side of the hedge, waiting impatiently—after all, the Penderwicks were leaving Arundel at the end of the week—until the Garden Club competition had come and gone. They shot lots of rubber-tipped arrows, they practiced soccer, they even played hide-and-seek when desperate, until finally the competition day itself arrived. Now all they had to do was stay away from the gardens for one more day, let Mrs. Tifton win her prize from Sir What's-his-name, and then all would be back to normal.

"You're late. You were supposed to be here for breakfast," said Skye to Jeffrey, who had just arrived. She and Jane were sitting on the cottage porch.

"We saved you some." Jane pointed to a plate of cold blueberry pancakes.

"I had to wait until I could sneak this out of the house," said Jeffrey, pulling a pamphlet out of his pocket and handing it to Skye.

"Pencey Military Academy. Where Boys Become Men and Men Become Soldiers," said Skye, reading from the pamphlet.

"Look at that poor kid." Jane pointed to a photograph of a young boy standing stiff as a ramrod in a tight blue military uniform.

"And check out the list of courses on the back," said Jeffrey. "There's no music except for the brass marching band. I'd die there. Go nuts and die."

"Darn that Dexter. Double darn that lousy rotten no-good creep," said Skye.

Rosalind and Batty came out onto the porch just in time to catch the end of Skye's outburst.

"Talking about Dexter again?" said Rosalind.

"Obviously," said Jane.

"Grrr," said Skye.

"I've been thinking. It's not that I mind going away to school, especially after Mother marries Dexter." Jeffrey shuddered. "But why not send me where I'd be happy? I know a kid whose sister goes to boarding school in Boston just so she can take viola classes at the New England Conservatory of Music on Saturdays. I'd really like something like that."

"Jeffrey, you've simply got to talk to your mother about this," said Rosalind.

"How can I?" Jeffrey cried out. "She hasn't even told me about marrying Dexter yet."

"Grrr," said Skye again.

"Poor Jeffrey." Batty put her little hand on his cheek. "Rosalind and I are going to hunt for dandelion leaves for Yaz and Carla, because rabbits love dandelion leaves, Cagney says. Come with us. It'll be fun."

"He can't," said Skye. "We need him for soccer."

"Another time, Battycakes," said Jeffrey.

"Skye and Jane, make sure you stay on this side of the hedge for the next several hours," said Rosalind. "Churchie called to remind us that the Garden Club people are arriving soon."

"You already told us that," said Skye.

"I'm telling you again. Daddy's keeping Hound inside with him at least until after lunch. We can't go into the gardens until we're sure those people are gone. Okay?" No one answered. Skye and Jane were studying the Pencey pamphlet, and Jeffrey was moodily devouring cold blueberry pancakes. Rosalind raised her voice. "SKYE! JANE! Make sure you stay away from Arundel Hall until the Garden Club competition is over! And don't forget about being ladies, or gentlemen, or whatever."

"We know, Rosalind," said Jane.

"Really we do," said Jeffrey.

"We've been good for days," said Skye. "We wouldn't be stupid enough to mess it up now."

"Because Mrs. Tifton—" said Rosalind.

"We'll be fine. Don't worry about it."

"Come on, Rosalind." Batty tugged at her hand. "We promised Cagney."

And Rosalind let Batty pull her away.

"Listen," said Jane, her nose still in the pamphlet. "At Pencey, we build strong moral character through hard work, strict discipline, and rigorous physical activity."

"I can't stand any more of that." Jeffrey snatched the pamphlet and threw it onto the porch. "Let's play soccer."

It was Skye's turn to pick the drill. She chose two-on-one slaughter, a combination of cross-country running, guerrilla warfare, and monkey-in-the-middle, perfect for rough terrain like the land around the cottage, with all its trees and long grasses. It was even better with two balls, which they now had, as Mr. Penderwick had repaired the one bitten by Hound. Jeffrey's ball had been christened Dexter days ago. Now Skye spat on the other one, officially naming it Pencey Military Academy, and kicked it into the air. Two-on-one slaughter had begun.

Jeffrey was a wild man that day, attacking the balls with a fury the other two had not yet seen. He gained control of the Pencey ball every chance he got and slammed it into trees, over rocks, anything he could find, until the girls thought the ball would explode. Not that Skye was all that civilized. Her blood was boiling over

Jeffrey's possible fate, and while she couldn't punish Dexter for his part in it, she certainly could punish the Dexter ball. But Jane was the worst of the three. The combination of worry about Jeffrey and two-on-one slaughter brought out her most aggressive side, so much so that she needed to become someone a lot tougher than herself, tougher even than Sabrina Starr, to get through it. That's where Mick Hart came in. Mick Hart, the oh-so-talented center from Manchester, England, dreamt up by Jane six months earlier after a terrible game in which she was pummeled by a fullback twice her size. When Jane was Mick, she felt no pain, she could maneuver around any fullback on the face of the earth, she was adored by fans and teammates alike, and she had a big mouth. The big mouth was Jane's favorite part.

"FISH HEAD!" she shouted over and over. "KNAVE! CHURL!"

For a while, Skye was working too hard to care about the insults. Tripped by a jutting tree root, she fumbled, ended up as the monkey without a ball, then had to struggle mightily to intercept either Dexter or Pencey as they whizzed by her again and again. But Jane and Jeffrey were both at the top of their game, and the balls eluded her, and her frustration grew.

"What's the matter, Skye?" taunted Jeffrey, neatly kicking Dexter over her head to Jane.

"Not a thing!" Skye spun around, just missing Pencey as it zipped past on its way to Jeffrey.

160

"GOOSEBERRY LOUSE!" shouted Jane with great glee. "SILLY GIT!"

Finally that was too much. Being called a fish head is one thing, but no one can stand being called a silly git by her younger sister, even when she doesn't know what a git is. Skye tossed away all the rules—not that there were that many rules—and faked a bad fall to the ground. Jane hesitated, sisterly love overcoming Mick Hart's ferocity for a split second, and Skye, laughing demonically, was suddenly on her feet and throwing herself at Pencey. She walloped the ball toward Jeffrey.

"Jane's the monkey!" she shouted triumphantly.

Again they were off! Dashing, darting, weaving, panting, Skye and Jeffrey passed Dexter and Pencey back and forth between them. And again. And again. And again. Jane, shouting, whooping, threatening, made dive after dive, until finally, inspired, she made a stunning leap into the air and stopped Dexter with a textbook foot trap.

Now Jeffrey was monkey. He positioned himself between the two sisters, determined to get back into the game. But Jane and Skye were suddenly the perfect team. On and on they dribbled, through the trees, exchanging the two balls with precision passes, keeping them away from him. It was two-on-one slaughter at its best—even Jeffrey, in his fury, could see that. But he wasn't going to let it go on. He decided to ignore

161

the balls that kept whizzing past his feet and charged straight at Skye.

"SKYE! DANGER!" shouted Jane, lobbing Dexter high into the air.

Skye saw Jeffrey coming at her and booted Pencey after Dexter.

Up flew the two balls together, higher and higher and higher, while below them, the players charged forward. Then just when it seemed that the balls would keep going until they reached the sky, Pencey and Dexter paused, hovered—

And began their slow, graceful descent over the top of the hedge and into the gardens.

Did anyone think then about the Garden Club competition? Did anyone hesitate, vaguely remembering what they'd been told over and over—stay out of the gardens that day? No, no one thought or hesitated, not for an instant. Frantic and bloodthirsty savages, all three zoomed to the tunnel and piled through, with Jane yelling war cries for everyone. COME TO ME, PENCEY BALL! COME TO MICK! UP PENDER-WICKS! DOWN DEXTER!

And once through, when they still had a chance to save themselves, did anyone listen for the approaching murmur of voices? Did anyone notice the glimpses of color moving along behind the rose arbor? Did anyone do anything sensible at all? Again, no. They had ears only for Jane's shouting and eyes only for the soccer balls landing—still in perfect synchronization—in front of the marble thunderbolt man, then bouncing and bouncing again, heading directly for the urn where Skye had hidden on her first day. An urn now full of glorious, lush, blooming pink jasmine.

Toward the urn the three children raced in a dead heat, Jane still shouting. FOR CHURCHILL, NELSON, AND PRINCE WILLIAM! Faster they ran and faster, until finally, magnificently, all three players and both balls smashed into the urn at exactly the same moment, splattering jasmine and dirt in all directions, before collapsing to the ground in one glorious, ecstatic, and very dirty mess.

"Now, that was a game of two-on-one slaughter," breathed Jane with great satisfaction.

"Amen," said Jeffrey.

Skye was the only one to sense the approaching danger. Maybe—she said this later—it was because she was the OAP, or maybe she at long last remembered the Garden Club, but for whatever reason, some instinct made her turn her head.

High heels, that's what she saw. A pair of navy blue high heels and, a little higher up, a white pleated linen skirt with a bit of crushed pink jasmine clinging to the hem. And that wasn't all. Next to the high heels was a pair of man's leather loafers, much too classy—too European—for Dexter to wear. And still that wasn't all, for behind the high heels and loafers were yet more

163

high heels. A whole platoon's worth of high heels. A whole army's worth.

"Jeffrey." Skye spoke softly but with great urgency.

He was too busy poking Jane to pay attention. "What *is* a git, anyway?"

"A git is a—"

"Jeffrey," said Skye again, staring helplessly at the hordes of advancing shoes. "Jane."

"—thoroughly useless person. Isn't it a great word? I found it in Daddy's *Oxford English Dictionary*." Jane put on Mick Hart's thick accent. "I say, that bloke Dexter is most definitely a—"

Skye slapped her hand over Jane's mouth. "Hello, Mrs. Tifton," she said in a desperate display of bravado. "How's the competition going?"

There had been bad moments at Arundel and there were more to come, but the total badness of this moment lived in the girls' memories for a long time. They and Jeffrey untangled themselves and struggled to their feet feeling like they were about to face a firing squad, one that had every right to shoot them. For they were completely in the wrong, and whatever anger and punishment the firing squad—that is, Mrs. Tifton—wanted to mete out, they deserved it.

Yet when they were upright and facing Mrs. Tifton, she didn't say the terrible things she must be thinking. Her face was dreadful to see—the fury, humiliation, and frustration, it was all there—but she was silent.

For this was all in her face, too—that if she tried to speak, she would yell, and if she yelled, she wouldn't be able to stop yelling, which absolutely could not happen in front of Sir Barnaby Patterne and the Garden Club. It was an epic struggle for Mrs. Tifton, and Skye and Jane would almost have felt sorry for her if they weren't too busy being frightened.

Then someone chuckled. It was a man's chuckle, and everyone looked away from Mrs. Tifton and toward Sir Barnaby. To their surprise, he had quite a nice face, with a friendly smile and lots of laugh wrinkles around his eyes.

"My son plays football—your soccer, you know—at his school in England. Too bad I didn't bring him along." He turned to Mrs. Tifton. "Are all these charming children yours?"

He had made it worse, and the Penderwicks were still debating years later whether or not he'd done it on purpose. Mrs. Tifton's conflict became visibly so much more painful that Skye was afraid she'd explode right there. Then for the first time Skye felt a—fleeting—twinge of admiration for the woman, as somehow she pulled herself together and turned calmly to Sir Barnaby.

"Jeffrey is my son. The girls are—" She stopped, unable to find a polite enough word.

"Friends," finished Jeffrey. "Skye and Jane Penderwick."

"We're renters," said Jane. "Mere renters at the

165

cottage here at Arundel, that is, our father is the renter and we are two of his four daughters, and we're awfully sorry about this mess, but I was wondering if being English and therefore from England, you've ever seen a World Cup—"

Skye kicked Jane to silence her. "We should go. We'll just clean up the jasmine first."

"Leave it," said Mrs. Tifton sharply. Her self-control was almost gone.

"Well, good luck with the competition, Mrs. Tifton. It was nice meeting you, Mr. Sir Patterne, and hello to all of you, too." Skye nodded to the rest of the Garden Club, some of whom—she was relieved to see—looked as though they were trying not to laugh. "Come on, Jane."

But Jane in her panic was still staring at Sir Barnaby—he was the least scary adult present, besides being English and therefore fascinating—and hadn't heard a word. In the end, Skye had to take her hand and drag her away. They waved to Jeffrey as they went, hoping they weren't leaving him to be maimed or murdered or worse. Feeling the eyes of thousands boring into their backs, they ran like the wind to the tunnel, ducked, and scuttled to safety. If Skye could have kicked herself at the same time, she would have. What fools they'd been to forget about the Garden Club competition. Stupid fools! Stupid! STUPID!

* * *

"Do you think Mrs. Tifton and all those other people heard that stuff I shouted?" asked Jane. It was evening of the same day, and she and Skye were once again sitting on the cottage porch. On the lawn in front of them, Rosalind and Batty were chasing fireflies.

"Are you nuts? People in Connecticut must have heard you," said Skye.

Jane groaned. "I hope we didn't get Jeffrey into too much trouble."

"Ha." Skye knew there was no chance Jeffrey wasn't in lots and lots of trouble.

Batty ran up, her hands cupped together. "I caught one named Horatio," she said, and spread open her hands. A lightning bug balanced uncertainly on her thumb.

"Look, he's blinking," said Jane. "He's trying to tell us something in Morse code."

"What?" asked Batty.

"Please . . . let . . . me . . . go," said Jane.

The bug flew away.

"Now I can't put him in the jar with the other ones," said Batty.

"Good," said Jane. "Let's play something else. How about circus acrobats?"

Across the yard, Rosalind unscrewed the lid of Batty's jar and watched the imprisoned lightning bugs bump their way to freedom. When the last one took flight, she had a sudden weird crawly feeling on the

167

back of her neck. As she later wrote to Anna, it wasn't like spiders—or lightning bugs—that you want to brush away. It was more like the soft touch of fate's finger, announcing the arrival of something—or someone—special.

Rosalind stood up. Walking toward her through the soft evening light was a tall, smiling young man wearing a baseball cap. He looked, if possible, even more adorable than the last time she had seen him.

"Hi, Cagney," she said, and tried to screw the lid onto the jar backward.

"Here, let me." Cagney secured the lid with a quick twist. "I've got a message for your sisters."

"They're on the porch." As Rosalind walked across the lawn beside him, she lengthened her stride to match his and noted that the top of her head barely reached his shoulder.

On the porch, Batty was upside down, balancing on her hands while Jane held her ankles. Skye saw Cagney and Rosalind approach. "Any news about Jeffrey?"

"He's been in his room all afternoon and has to stay there until morning," said Cagney. "He asked me to come over and tell you he's fine."

"Does Mrs. Tifton have him on bread and water?" asked Jane.

"No, Churchie's got him on hamburgers, corn on the cob, and blueberry pie."

"Is he locked in? Does he have enough books to

read?" Jane paused while Skye whispered in her ear.
"Oh! Good idea! Rosalind, we're going for a walk."
She handed Batty's ankles over to Rosalind and
jumped off the porch with Skye.

"Don't be long. It's getting dark," said Rosalind as
they melted away into the trees.

"Nice kids," said Cagney.

"For their age."

"Mmphph," said Batty, still upside down.

"Looks like we might finally get some rain," Cagney
said. "The gardens sure need it."

"There hasn't been any rain at all since we got
here," said Rosalind.

"MMPHPH!" said Batty.

"Oh, my, I forgot about you."

"I'm right here!"

"I know you are. I'm sorry." Rosalind gently lowered Batty to the floor. "Why don't you go get the surprise for Cagney?"

Batty scampered inside. She was back in a minute
with a big plastic bag stuffed full of dandelion greens.
"Rosalind and I porridged these for Yaz and Carla."

"Foraged," said Rosalind. "But, Batty, I meant the
other surprise. The one we got in town with Daddy
yesterday."

"Oh, that." Batty went inside again. This time she
came back with a gift-wrapped package that she
handed to Cagney. "This is because I let Yaz escape. I

wanted to get you the rabbit calendar, but Rosalind said you'd like this better. She used up her allowance for the next two months on it, since she'd already spent all her money on Jeffrey's present."

"Shh," said Rosalind.

"A book of Civil War photographs!" said Cagney, tearing off the wrapping paper. "What a wonderful surprise! But you didn't have to."

"Yes, we did."

"You know, I think Batty did Yaz a favor. He's stopped trying to escape all the time. He won't even go near the door. But thanks, Rosalind. This was very thoughtful."

"Let's catch more lightning bugs," said Batty.

"It's time for you to get ready for bed," said Rosalind. "I'll be up there in a few minutes for a story."

"I need a bath first."

"You just had one last night."

"My feet are dirty again." Batty slid one foot out of its sandal and held it up between Rosalind and Cagney. It was indeed dirty.

"Okay, you need a bath," said Rosalind. "Ask Daddy to run the water for you, and I'll be inside soon to help with the rinsing and drying."

"I want you to run the water."

Rosalind glanced at Cagney. He was paging through his new book, holding it close to his eyes to see the pictures in the fading light. She gave him until the count of three to look away from the Civil War and over at her. One. Two. Three. She sighed and said, "We have to go inside now, Cagney. Good night."

Only then did he look at Rosalind. "Good night, and thanks again for the book and the dandelions."

Rosalind took Batty's hand and led her into the house.

"I still think he would have liked that rabbit calendar better," said Batty.

"Thank goodness Cagney installed a rope ladder," said Skye to Jane. They were underneath the big tree outside Jeffrey's bedroom, and Skye was untying a length of twine from a nail hammered into the tree trunk. "Jeffrey showed me how it works the other day. This twine is keeping the ladder rolled up in the tree. You undo the knot, let go of the twine, and the ladder falls down. There's another knot up at the top if someone's trying to get down instead of up."

"Ouch!" The ladder had fallen on Jane's head.

"You aren't supposed to stand right under it."

"You could have told me that before."

"Climb."

They clambered to the top of the rope ladder and eased themselves carefully onto the lowest tree branch, the one where they had gotten stuck their first week at the cottage. Jane looked straight up. The daylight was gone, and thick clouds were hiding the moon and stars. All she could see were black branches against an almost-black sky.

"Scared to climb in the dark?" said Skye.

"Fear never stops Sabrina Starr."

"When we get further up, we'll have the light from Jeffrey's window." Skye pointed to a rectangle of light high up on the house.

"Hark, I hear music."

Skye tipped her head to listen. "It's Jeffrey."

"The boy poured his misery and loneliness into his beloved piano," said Jane. Good line, she thought, but too late for my book. She had already begun Sabrina Starr's rescue scene—complete with bow and arrow—and there was no way Arthur could take a piano along on that hot-air balloon ride. Of course, she could go back and add the misery and loneliness line to a previous chapter, but Jane hated to revise. She believed in sticking with her original creative vision.

"Climb," said Skye.

Slowly and carefully, they hauled themselves up the tree, higher and higher, until they reached the branch outside Jeffrey's window. They peered into his room. He was sitting slumped on the piano stool, no longer playing, just staring into space.

"Psst," said Jane.

He jumped up and ran to the window. "What are you doing here?"

"Cagney said you were okay, but we felt guilty and wanted to see you."

"We're really sorry," said Skye. "It was idiotic to forget about the competition."

"It wasn't your job to remember," said Jeffrey. "I live here."

"I guess so, but if we hadn't been distracting you, especially Jane with her dumb Mick Hart—"

"Honest, it's okay."

"It's not okay." Skye pulled the Pencey pamphlet out of her pocket and handed it to Jeffrey. "Anyway, you left this on the porch."

"I should have thrown it down the toilet," said Jeffrey. "Can you come inside?"

"We'd better not," said Skye. "It's late and Daddy will be looking for us soon."

"What did your mother say to you after all those people left?" asked Jane.

"She said—she yelled—all about how I don't care about her feelings anymore. I do care. She's my mother."

"We know," said Jane.

"Then she found out Arundel got second place in the competition and yelled at me all over again. Mrs. Robinette got first place," said Jeffrey. "That really killed Mother. She kept talking about me needing more discipline."

"She didn't say anything about going to Pencey this year, did she?" said Skye.

"No, but she hinted that she and Dexter have a lot to talk about tonight."

"That doesn't sound good."

Jeffrey turned his head, listening. "I hear someone coming. You'd better go."

"See you tomorrow morning?" said Jane.

"At the cottage," said Jeffrey. "Do or die."

CHAPTER THIRTEEN
The Piano Lesson

"THIS IS LOUSY," SAID SKYE, looking out the window at the pouring rain. The four sisters were in the cottage kitchen. Jane and Batty were finishing up their breakfast, and Rosalind was making brownies again.

"The gardens sure need it, though," said Rosalind.

"Why couldn't it have rained yesterday instead, when the Garden Club was here? Then we wouldn't have been playing soccer and we wouldn't have gone through the hedge," said Skye.

"You wouldn't have gone through the hedge if you'd listened to me," said Rosalind.

"Oh, Rosalind, don't. We're worried enough without you rubbing it in," said Jane.

"I'm not worried," said Skye. She was fibbing. The

Penderwicks were going home to Cameron in three days. How could that possibly be enough time to help Jeffrey out of the trouble they'd gotten him into? If they even could help. Oh, where was he?

"Achoo," sneezed Jane.

"Yuch, you spit on my cereal," said Batty.

Rosalind swept the tainted cereal bowl away from Batty with one hand and felt Jane's forehead with the other. "You feel like you have a fever, Jane."

"I'm fine, really."

"Jeffrey's here!" Skye threw open the door. "Thank goodness you made it."

"I said I would." He shrugged off his rain-drenched jacket.

"We were afraid you'd still be locked up," said Jane.

"Mother let me come out of my room this morning, and then she and Dexter left for Vermont to shop for antiques. So I'm free."

"ACHOO!" said Jane.

"YUCH!" said Batty.

"Jane, go upstairs to your room and rest," said Rosalind.

"I don't want to rest," said Jane.

"You don't have a choice," said Rosalind. "Go upstairs to your bedroom."

"Sabrina Starr always obeys orders. But I won't rest. I'll work on my book. It's almost finished. Isn't that exciting?"

"Very exciting," said Jeffrey.

"Good-bye, Jeffrey. Don't let Skye get you into any more trouble," said Jane.

"Me?" said Skye. "At least I won't turn into Mick Hart."

"Sabrina Starr departed with dignity." Jane sneezed three times, each sneeze bigger than the last, then left for her bedroom.

"What should we do?" Skye asked Jeffrey. "I wanted to practice with the bows and arrows again, but we can't in the rain."

"I have an idea of something we can do at my house," said Jeffrey. "But it's a surprise and I'm not going to tell you what it is until we get there. Would you like to come, too, Rosalind?"

"I'll stay here, in case Jane needs anything," said Rosalind. "I have a book about the Battle of Gettysburg I want to read, anyway."

"Cagney lent it to her," said Skye to Jeffrey. "She already whipped through his oh-so-fascinating one about Civil War generals."

"Yawn," said Jeffrey.

Rosalind ignored them.

"Can I come with you, Jeffrey?" said Batty.

"Sure," said Jeffrey.

"No," said Skye.

"How much trouble can she be?"

"You'll find out."

"Can we take carrots to Yaz and Carla first? And then can we stop by the lily pond to visit the frogs?" said Batty.

"Oh, Batty." Jeffrey looked helplessly at Skye.

"Be tough."

"Rabbits, yes, frogs, no," said Jeffrey.

"Cool. I was sure you'd say no to both," said Batty, and dove into the refrigerator for carrots.

"This is your big idea, Jeffrey? Teaching me how to play the piano?" said Skye. They were in the music room at Arundel Hall and she was staring with dismay at the grand piano in the corner. It was the biggest piano she had ever seen. Right now, with the threat looming of having to make music on it, it seemed like the biggest thing she had ever seen, period. Like a black, shiny whale ready to eat her up with embarrassment.

"You'll like it. Music is a lot like math. You're good at math, right?" said Jeffrey.

"I'm excellent at math and my clarinet was nothing like that at all. It was torture. Let's go up into the attic again. There's tons of stuff up there to mess around with."

"Coward."

"I'm not a coward." Skye made a ferocious, uncowardly face at him.

"Then just try it. It'll be fun, I promise."

"Couldn't we at least use the piano in your room? It isn't so big."

"There's only a stool up there. We couldn't both sit." Jeffrey sat down on one side of the piano bench and patted the empty space next to him. "Come on."

Gingerly, Skye squeezed herself behind the piano and lowered herself onto the bench. She felt trapped. In back of her was a corner with no door or window. In front of her was the gigantic piano with its eighty-eight teeth and soaring lid. She couldn't even see past it into the rest of the room.

"Okay, now listen for a minute," said Jeffrey, shaking the tension out of his hands, then lowering them to the keys.

Before Jeffrey could strike a note, Batty's head popped up on his side of the piano bench. Skye jumped. The little squirt must have crawled under the piano to get there.

"Hey, Jeffrey," said Batty. "Can I play with those pillows on the couch?"

"Sure," he said. Batty's head disappeared.

"What pillows?" said Skye.

"Don't worry about it. Close your eyes and listen," said Jeffrey, and played several bars of music. "Now, that was Bach. Did you hear the mathematical progressions?"

"Of course not. Let's explore the basement today. I love basements."

Batty's head appeared next to Jeffrey again. "Can I play with that gold thing by the fireplace?"

"You mean the fire screen? Go ahead," said Jeffrey, and Batty's head vanished.

"You're letting her play with gold?" said Skye.

"Don't worry, it's only brass. Now concentrate. You must already know from playing the clarinet—"

"*Trying* to play the clarinet."

"—that notes are like fractions. Whole notes, halves, quarters, eighths, sixteenths. That's math. But you can also think of the scale as a base-eight number system. Do, re, mi, fa, so, la, ti, then we get to eight and have to start over again with do, right? Listen." Jeffrey played a scale on the piano.

Once again, there was Batty beside Jeffrey. "What about those little stone animals on the table in the corner?" she said.

"Play with whatever you want," said Jeffrey. "Just be careful."

"Okay," she said, and left.

"Skye, listen to the music. Hear the patterns."

"You're not going to give up, are you?"

"I really think you could be good at this if you would just try." He played the piece again. This time he went past the first measures and continued to the end. When he finished, he looked expectantly at Skye.

"Huh, you know, I think I'm starting to get it."

"Really?"

180

"It's all about combining logic and instinct. Let me try," she said, shaking out her hands, then lowering them gracefully to the keyboard. CRASH! BANG! DISCORD! BOOM!

"Stop! You win! Be quiet!" he shouted, covering his ears, but Skye was enjoying herself too much to stop. So Jeffrey started to tickle her and kept on doing it until Skye fell off her side of the piano bench. Only then was blessed silence restored.

Jeffrey looked down at Skye on the floor. "Now we can discuss the key of E-flat."

Skye lunged at him and yanked him off the bench. The tickling began again. There was lots of hysterical laughter, that is, in between the shouted threats. Tickling turned to wrestling then to pummeling. The piano bench was kicked over and sheet music flew everywhere.

So loud was the joyful mayhem that neither heard the sound of someone opening the door and coming into the room. Had they been more careful—but why would they have been? They couldn't have known that Dexter's car would get a flat tire on the way to Vermont and that he would get so wet and dirty changing it in the rain that he'd turn around and bring Mrs. Tifton home early. And they certainly couldn't have known that she'd hear their thumping and laughing from the hall and come in to see what was going on. But that's what happened, and this time Sir

Barnaby wasn't there to keep Mrs. Tifton from losing her temper out loud.

"You again!" She glared venomously down at Skye. "YOU!"

Jeffrey lurched to his feet, knocking the fallen piano bench into the piano leg in the process. "Mother," he gasped. "I thought you were in Vermont."

"And this is how you take advantage of my absence—rolling around like a hooligan with this obnoxious—this wretched—"

Skye stood up beside Jeffrey, unashamed—for they hadn't been doing anything wrong. Today there was no spilled urn, no splattered jasmine, no ruined competition. "I started the rolling around, Mrs. Tifton."

"Oh, I wouldn't doubt for a minute that you started it, Jane. You cause havoc wherever you go. First my poor garden, and now this!" said Mrs. Tifton, indicating the rest of the music room with a dramatic sweep of her arm.

Skye and Jeffrey peered around the grand piano. Oh, no, thought Skye. Maybe there wasn't a spilled urn, but something pretty awful had been added to the music room—a sort of combination Wild West fort and Arabian Nights tent, built from couch pillows and a brass fire screen, plus a dozen large leather-covered books and several elegant silk throws.

"Batty?"

A pale and frightened face peeked out from behind *Vanity Fair*.

"It's all right," said Jeffrey. "You don't have to hide."

Batty crawled into view. In each of her hands was a small, intricately carved stone lion.

"Papa's African sculptures!" said Mrs. Tifton. "Jeffrey Framley Tifton, have you no respect for anything of mine?"

"He was just—" said Skye.

Mrs. Tifton turned on her, cutting her off. "Leave my house, you and your sister both. The Penderwicks are no longer welcome here."

"Mother, they—" said Jeffrey.

"I will not hear another word from you until they are gone," said Mrs. Tifton.

"Then I'll show them out," he said staunchly.

"I'm sure they know the way. You will stay here and help me clear up this disaster."

"It's okay," said Skye to Jeffrey. "We do know the way. Come on, Batty, let's go."

Batty carefully placed the little sculptures on the floor, then crept over to Skye, using her under-the-piano detour to avoid Mrs. Tifton.

"See you later," said Jeffrey.

"Yes. I'll see you later, Jeffrey. Thank you for teaching me how to play the piano," said Skye, and, with her head held high, marched past Mrs. Tifton and out the door.

Batty made it out of the music room before she started to cry, but when her tears did come, they were what Mr. Penderwick called Batty's silent storm, that is, fast, furious, and without any noise. Skye pulled her down the hall to where they couldn't be heard by Mrs. Tifton.

"Don't. Not now." Calming Batty wasn't one of Skye's talents. She wished Rosalind were there or even Jane.

"It's all my fault." Batty's wings drooped and her tears flowed like waterfalls. "I shouldn't have come, Skye, like you said."

There was no comfort in saying I told you so, not with Batty already crying like her heart would break. And besides, Skye knew this was much more her own fault than Batty's.

"I'm the OAP," she said. "I should have been paying more attention."

"I guess so."

"Then stop crying and dry your face."

"I don't have a tissue," sobbed Batty. This new tragedy only made her cry harder.

"Use your clothes. I won't tell anyone."

While Batty scrubbed at her face with her little shirt, Skye looked anxiously back toward the music room. She desperately wanted to eavesdrop—just for a moment— to make sure Jeffrey wasn't getting too horribly punished.

"I'm done," said Batty. Her shirt was very wet and

crumpled-looking now, but her tears had slowed to a trickle.

"Good job." Skye awkwardly patted her head. "Now go to the kitchen. Churchie will give you something to eat."

"I want to stay with you. Please."

Any minute Mrs. Tifton could come bursting out of the music room. It was either listen at the door right now or leave the house altogether. And Skye just couldn't bear to leave without knowing that Jeffrey was all right. Especially not after getting him into trouble yet again.

"Okay," she said. "But you must be very quiet while I check on Jeffrey."

"You mean you're going to snoop."

"Yes, snoop, and if you don't like it, you can go find Churchie now."

Batty preferred snooping to wandering around Arundel Hall by herself, so the two sisters tiptoed back to the music room and pressed their ears to the door. Mrs. Tifton was talking.

"I don't understand what's happened, Jeffrey. You never used to defy me this way. Ever since those Penderwicks—"

"It's got nothing to do with them, Mother," said Jeffrey.

"You used to have such nice friends, like Teddy Robinette."

"Teddy Robinette's never been my friend. He's a bully and a jerk."

"I don't believe this."

"No one at school likes him and he cheats. You just wanted me to be his friend because he's from a rich fam—"

"That's enough!" Skye and Batty could hear Mrs. Tifton pacing. "I just don't know how to handle you anymore. Dexter's been saying you need a firmer hand. Maybe he's right."

"Dexter!" said Jeffrey scornfully.

"What does that mean? You don't like him, either? If not, you'd better say something right now, because—" She broke off in the middle of her sentence.

"Because you're going to marry him?" said Jeffrey.

The pacing stopped and Mrs. Tifton's voice became softer, almost pleading. "Would that be so bad? For me to have a husband? And you a father?"

"He doesn't want to be my father! He wants to get rid of me by sending me away to Pencey a whole year early!"

"We're still discussing—" Suddenly her soft and pleading tone was gone. "Just a minute, young man. How do you know about that?"

"Well—we—I—heard you talking about it."

"We?" There was a long pause. "Answer me, Jeffrey. When and with whom did you spy on me? Does Churchie have something to do with this? Cagney?"

186

"No, no," he cried. "Of course not."

"Those Penderwicks, then. I should have known."

"But we weren't spying, Mother. Really we weren't. We heard you and Dexter talking by mistake after my birthday party."

"By mistake, was it? I'll bet the spying was Jane's idea. Sneaky, sarcastic blonde."

"You mean Skye, and she's not—"

"Don't interrupt," Mrs. Tifton snapped. "And it's not only Jane—Skye. It's all of them. They're uncouth, rude, and conceited. This is what happens when parents don't do their jobs. The father's a pushover, and who knows where the mother ran off to. I suppose she got tired of caring for all those girls. I certainly would."

For the two in the hallway, this was a nightmare. Skye didn't mind being called sneaky and sarcastic. That wasn't so awful, considering the source, and it was true that here she was, spying. But to hear Mrs. Tifton criticize her father and, worse—oh, much worse—spew out nasty ideas about her mother. It was unbearable. Skye felt a red rage building inside her. Her hands tightened into hard fists. Her ears rang so that she could just barely hear Jeffrey's reply.

"Mother, Mrs. Penderwick—"

"And that Rosalind is always chasing after Cagney like a lovesick puppy. If she keeps up that kind of behavior, one of these days some man will allow himself to be caught, and that will be the end of her wide-eyed innocence. Plus you can't tell me there's nothing wrong with the little one. Those tacky wings and the odd way she stares without speaking—"

Skye knew she shouldn't go in there. It wasn't gentlemanly, and it would only give Mrs. Tifton more reason to hate her. Yes, she knew all that, and even Batty was tugging at her arm to keep her from doing it. But it didn't matter. The family—her mother's!—honor was at stake, and she had to defend the people she loved the best. She took a deep breath, girded herself for battle, and threw open the door and charged across the room toward Mrs. Tifton.

"Where—what—" sputtered Mrs. Tifton.

"You can't talk about my family like that!" shouted Skye. "Take it back now!"

"How dare you! In my home!" Mrs. Tifton ran to the door and shouted into the hallway. "Churchie! Come to the music room right now!"

Skye followed her. "I dare because I'm a Penderwick. But you wouldn't know anything about that!"

"Jeffrey, you see! She was spying again!"

"I was spying, I admit it," said Skye proudly. "I needed to make sure Jeffrey was all right."

"Make sure—you presumptuous—CHURCHIE!"

"And I'm glad I spied because I heard those things you said and you couldn't—"

Skye felt a soothing hand on her shoulder. It was Churchie, flushed and panting from running.

"Come, Skye." Churchie picked up Batty, who was crying all over again. "You'd better go back to the cottage now."

But Skye was too far gone to listen. She stuck her face up close to Mrs. Tifton's. "You couldn't in a million years understand anything about my mother. You're not good enough. She would never have left us on purpose. She died. Did you hear me? My mother is DEAD!"

"I didn't know—no one told me—"

"Jeffrey was trying to tell you, but you wouldn't pay attention, just like you never—"

"Skye, that's enough, dear." It was Churchie again. "Tend to your sister."

"Yes, Churchie, please." Mrs. Tifton looked like she was going to faint. "Get her away from me."

"I'll get myself away," said Skye. Still shaking with anger, she went over to Jeffrey. He was shaking, too, not from anger, but as if he'd barely survived a tornado. Skye lowered her voice so that only he could hear. "I'm sorry. I'm so sorry. I had to, though."

"I know."

She made her hand into a fist and held it out to him. He put his fist on top of hers.

"Friends forever?" said Skye.

"Friends forever."

"Penderwick Family Honor," they said together.

* * *

Skye stalked through the rain, feeling it running down her hair and face and into her T-shirt and shorts, soaking them. After tucking Batty into her yellow slicker, Churchie had tried to get Skye into a raincoat, too, but she'd been too impatient to get out of the house and as far away from Mrs. Tifton as possible. Now they were almost to the marble thunderbolt man. Soon they'd be through the tunnel and back on the sane, peaceful side of the hedge.

"I have a question." Batty was peering up from under the brim of her rain hat.

"What?"

"Am I odd? Is there something wrong with me, like Mrs. Tifton said?"

Skye knelt down on the wet grass and looked right into Batty's eyes. "No, you stupid idiot, there's nothing wrong with you. You're perfect. Mrs. Tifton doesn't know what she's talking about."

"Are you sure?"

"Absolutely positive."

"Oh," said Batty.

"Do you have any more questions?"

"Not right now."

"Then let's get you home to Daddy." Skye took hold of Batty's hand and held it all of the way back to the cottage.

CHAPTER FOURTEEN
A Midnight Adventure

"ONE MORE STORY," said Batty.

"You've already had three," said Rosalind. "You know the rule is one story at bedtime."

"Please, Rosalind. Hound is lonely and sad tonight."

Hound dropped the bone he had been chewing, galloped across the room, and leapt joyously onto Batty's bed.

"Yes, he looks lonely and sad," said Rosalind, pushing Hound off the bed and wondering for the fifteenth time what had happened to Skye and Batty at Arundel Hall that morning. Skye had locked herself in her room the moment she got back to the cottage. Batty's eyes had been red and swollen, and she'd insisted on sticking close to Rosalind for the rest of the day. Neither would say what was wrong.

"Tell me a story about Mommy and Uncle Gordon when they were little," said Batty.

"All right, one more story if you promise to go to sleep afterward."

"I promise."

"Do you want peanut-butter-on-the-walls or the bobsled?"

"Both."

"Batty—" said Rosalind warningly.

"The bobsled."

Rosalind began, "When Uncle Gordon was seven years old and Mommy was five, Uncle Gordon read a book about bobsledding and decided he wanted to learn how."

"But it was summer."

"And there was no snow. So Uncle Gordon took the mattress off his bed and dragged it to the top of the stairs so he could slide it down like a bobsled. But he wasn't sure how well it would work, so he told Mommy to take the first ride."

"Mommy said no," said Batty sleepily. Her eyes were starting to close.

"Until Uncle Gordon said he'd pay her twenty-five cents to do it. So Mommy got under the covers—Uncle Gordon had left the sheets and blankets on the mattress to make it more like a bobsled—and Uncle

Gordon gave the whole thing a giant push." Rosalind paused a minute and, when Batty didn't chime in, went on in a whisper. "But it wasn't a straight staircase. After twelve steps, it came to a landing where it curved around, then went down another twelve steps. So, of course, when the mattress got to the landing, it got stuck and folded up like an accordion, and Mommy was all tangled up in blankets and sheets and mattress, and she started to yell—Batty?"

Batty had finally fallen asleep. Rosalind tucked her in securely, kissed her cheek, and gave Hound a stern stay-off-the-bed look. He gave her back a big red doggy grin full of innocence and the promise to never even think about jumping on Batty's bed ever again. Rosalind turned off the light, closed the door behind her, and heard a great thump. She sighed and headed for the steps to the attic.

Now it was time to go upstairs to check on Jane, who had stayed in bed all day with her cold, napping, then writing, then reading, then napping again. Jane's light was on, and the book she had been reading, *Magic by the Lake*, was lying open on the bedcovers. But Jane was fast asleep, her uncombed curls scattered across the pillow. Rosalind moved the book to the bedside table, then brushed her fingers against Jane's forehead—it was cooler. The fever had dropped. Daddy would be relieved.

Jane stirred and muttered, "Now that you are free,

Arthur, whither shall I convey you in my balloon? Choose your heart's desire. Where shall it be? Russia? Australia? Brasilia?"

"Jane, it's Rosalind. Do you need anything?"

"And the boy replied, 'Anywhere in the world where Ms. Horriferous can't find me.' "

"Shh, go back to sleep." Rosalind turned off the light, then slipped downstairs and into her own room.

Only three more nights, she thought, then home to Cameron. Would she miss this room? It wasn't as pretty as her room at home, with its cherry furniture and the colorful plaid curtains and bedspread her mother had made. But still, she had been happy here. There was Cagney's book about Gettysburg on the bed—she was almost finished with it. And a white rose from his Fimbriata bush on the bureau. And all the letters she had gotten so far from Anna, filled with advice about Cagney. And hanging on the outside of the closet door, where Rosalind could look at it every day, the striped dress she'd worn to Jeffrey's birthday party. Rosalind walked over and touched the covered buttons on the back, one at a time. Thirteen of them. She knew that by heart, just like she knew by heart what Cagney said when he saw her in it.

Rosalind wandered over to the window and looked out. The rain had stopped, and the sky had cleared—the moon was riding high above the treetops. Rosalind pushed up the screen and leaned out the window.

She'd calculated that by pitching herself at a certain angle and twisting a little to the left, she was pointed directly at Cagney's apartment and would even have been able to see its lights if those trees and the hedge hadn't been in the way.

"Wow, you girls look great." That's what he'd said. Once in a while she allowed herself to pretend he'd been talking only to her. "Wow, Rosalind, you look—"

She jumped, hitting her head on the bottom of the screen. Somebody was knocking on her bedroom door.

"Rosalind? Are you in there?"

It was Skye. Rosalind quietly pushed the screen into place and opened the door. "What's wrong?"

"Nothing's wrong. Why does something have to be wrong?" said Skye. She came in and sat down on the bed.

"Fine, nothing's wrong. You always lock yourself in your bedroom for hours, then act like a grumpy bear at supper."

"Was I that bad?"

"Yes." Rosalind sat down, too, and waited. It was usually easier to let Skye go at her own speed.

She took a while. First she looked all around the room, swinging her legs, and then she stared at the ceiling for a few minutes. Finally she said, "Do you ever lose your temper?"

"I yelled at you about those cookies you burnt when we first got here."

195

"No, I mean really, really lose it and go kind of nuts."

"When Tommy Geiger dumped my book report in a mud puddle on purpose, I called him terrible names and everything."

"Rosalind, that was years ago! Like third or fourth grade!"

"Well, that's the last time I can remember."

Skye went back to looking at the ceiling. Rosalind's patience was running low. If she didn't push Skye a little, they could be sitting here all night.

"Did you lose your temper today?"

"Yes, how did you know? I lost my temper at Mrs. Tifton. I said things—" Skye stopped. "But the things she said first. Terrible things. I couldn't help it."

Rosalind was sure that she should reprimand Skye. Penderwicks didn't lose their tempers at adults, especially after they'd promised to behave well to those very same adults. But the idea of Mrs. Tifton saying terrible things sent a chill down her back. She had to ask.

"What terrible things?"

"About Mommy."

It was like a slap in the face. Rosalind gasped and glanced over at the photograph of her mother on her bedside table. Her beloved mother, worlds and universes better than Mrs. Tifton. "How could she? What does she know about Mommy?"

"Nothing. She was all wrong and I told her so."

"Good for you."

"So you don't think I was wrong to lose my temper?"

"Well—" Rosalind struggled with herself.

"Because she said terrible stuff about the rest of us, too. She said that I was sneaky and sarcastic and that Batty's odd and that you follow Cagney around like a lovesick puppy and someday a man will let himself be caught and that'll be the end of your innocence."

"The end of my—" This was worse than a slap. This was like having a pail of slimy, rotten garbage dumped over your head. Rosalind flung herself down and buried her face in the pillow.

Skye was aghast. Was there no end to the damage she could do with her big mouth? "I'm sorry, Rosalind. I should have kept it to myself."

"No, you were right to tell me. But please go away now. I need to be alone."

"But "

"Go."

You can't lie here forever, Rosalind told herself. Oh, yes, I can, she answered back. I can lie here for as long as I want, which is until it's time to get into the car and drive home to Cameron. That way I never have to see anyone from Arundel ever again. It probably isn't just Mrs. Tifton who knows what a fool I've been.

Churchie, creepy Dexter, Harry the Tomato Man. Maybe even Cagney.

Rosalind shifted restlessly on the bed. She had been lying there for two hours, doing nothing but listening to her thoughts go around and around. When Mr. Penderwick had come in to say good night, she had pretended to be asleep while he covered her with a blanket and turned out the light. She had never done that to him before. It seemed deceitful. Was that what being in love did to people?

Was she in love? She had asked herself that many times in the last few weeks. Anna's mother said you're in love when you feel like you've been hit by a truck. Rosalind felt bad enough for a motorcycle, maybe, but not a truck. Anyway, could you be in love with someone who didn't love you? And more important, someone you'd never kissed? Anna said no. Rosalind wasn't sure. She knew that you could kiss without being in love. She had certainly not been in love with Nate Cartmell when he kissed her at the Valentine's Day party or with Tommy Geiger when she pecked his cheek after losing that bet to Anna. But those had been passages from her childhood, she thought. Kissing Cagney would be very, very different.

Kissing Cagney. Just thinking those words made Rosalind blush and feel confused and giddy. This is awful, she thought. I'm turning into one of those girls at school who thinks only about boys. She sat up abruptly and tugged hard at her curls. I need some fresh air, she thought, something to clear my brain.

It was pleasantly wicked to be outside at midnight without anyone knowing where she was. Rosalind skipped through the still-wet grass, her face raised to the moon. How glorious and mysterious was the moon, hanging forever in the heavens. What was Mrs. Tifton and her nasty little mind compared to the moon? Nothing! Rosalind twirled around, as though she were again young and carefree.

She wanted to see the Arundel gardens one last time before she went back to hiding in her bedroom. She ran along the hedge, plunged through the tunnel, raced around the marble thunderbolt man, and came to a sudden halt, struck by the beauty of the place. The moonlight had turned the gardens into a fairyland, magnificent and mysterious. Fairyland? First twirling, then fairyland. What was wrong with her? Was she turning into Jane? Rosalind sprinted off at top speed. She must need more exercise.

By the time she got to the lily pond, she was out of breath. She flung herself down on a large rock that stuck out into the water and rolled over to look again at the sky. A million stars were twinkling down at her. She wondered what it would be like to be looking at the stars with Cagney there beside her. What would they talk about? Constellations? Rosalind had learned the constellations in fourth grade but could only remember Orion's belt. But maybe there would be no need for talk. Maybe they would hold hands and—

The fantasy vanished in a flash. Rosalind had heard something, and it wasn't one of the lily pond's frogs. It was a giggle.

She turned over and looked for the giggler and right away wished she had stayed hidden in her room. Across the pond stood two people gazing into each other's eyes. They hadn't been there a minute before. Rosalind prayed that they would go away, but no, there they stayed, aware of nothing but each other. Then Rosalind prayed that the tall boy in the baseball cap wasn't who she knew he was. The girl, a teenager with long red hair, Rosalind had never seen before and hoped never to see again.

I'll be okay, thought Rosalind, if only he doesn't kiss her.

He kissed her.

Now Rosalind felt like she had been hit by a truck. She needed to get out of there. Away, away, back to her bed and under the covers now, immediately. Without a sound, without breathing almost, she crept backward along the rock. One inch, another. Oh, no! She was too late. They had stopped kissing and were turning toward her. And here she was, pinned on top of this rock, shining in the moonlight like a giant white spider. She had to do something. If they saw her, her life was over. Maybe if she slithered down the side of the rock toward the water, she wouldn't be so obvious and they wouldn't see her. Slide, slither, slide, still unseen. Slither, slide, then—

"Oh, no!" yelped Rosalind, losing her balance. She fell with a loud splash into the lily pond.

"Is she all right?" This was a girl's voice that Rosalind had never heard before.

"She must have knocked her head pretty hard against the rock when she fell. We've got to try to keep her warm." Rosalind knew this voice. It belonged to a boy whose name she didn't want to remember right now. She felt him wrap something soft and dry around her. Only then did she realize that she was lying on the ground, that she was wet and cold, and that her head hurt like crazy.

"Do you know who she is?" said the girl.

"Rosalind, the oldest of those Penderwick sisters I told you about. Oh, man, she's starting to shiver."

"She's kind of pretty, don't you think?"

"I don't know, she's just a kid," said the boy. "Look, do you mind staying here with her for a few minutes? I've got to get Mr. Penderwick."

Rosalind stirred and groaned. She wanted to tell them not to bother her father, but when she opened her mouth, she said, "Too much of water hast thou, poor Ophelia."

"What the heck does that mean?" said the girl.

"I think she's delirious. Rosalind, can you hear me?" said Cagney, for of course that's who the boy was. Why couldn't a passing stranger have pulled her out of the pond?

She opened her eyes and commanded her brain to function properly. "Don't bother Daddy," she said.

"You hit your head," said Cagney.

"I'm okay, really," she said, and tried to sit up. She saw that she was covered by a Red Sox sweatshirt.

Cagney gently pushed her back down. "You shouldn't move yet."

"I want to go home," she said, and, to her disgust, started to cry.

"Then I'll carry you."

"No, no, I can walk," Rosalind protested, but Cagney scooped her up, Red Sox sweatshirt and all, and cradled her in his arms. She peeked over his shoulder at the red-headed girl. She's beautiful, thought Rosalind, and felt like a bedraggled sack of potatoes.

"This is Kathleen," said Cagney.

"Hi," said Rosalind.

"Sorry about your accident," said Kathleen.

Accident! Rosalind's whole summer felt like an accident right now.

"Okay, Rosy, hang on," said Cagney. "Here we go."

For many years afterward, Rosalind wouldn't be able to see a Red Sox sweatshirt without remembering that long, long trip back to the cottage. Kathleen chattered away about friends she and Cagney had in common—whom Rosalind had never met—and about a movie they'd seen together—a love story Rosalind had never heard of—and dates they'd been on before and dates they would go on later. Cagney threw in a comment here and there, but as for Rosalind, she didn't say anything, not one word the whole time. What could she say? That this was all unbearably humiliating, and that she hadn't known they would be at the lily pond, and that if she had known, it was the last place on earth she would've gone? No, she couldn't say any of those things, and she knew now that constellations and Orion's belt were much too stupid to mention. So she closed her eyes and rested her head on Cagney's shoulder—there was nowhere else to put it, and it did hurt so badly—and let the tears slide silently down her cheeks.

CHAPTER FIFTEEN
The Shredded Book

"**D**O YOU WANT TO TELL ME about last night, Rosalind?" said Mr. Penderwick.

"There's nothing to tell, Daddy, really. I needed some air, so I took a walk, fell into the lily pond, and hit my head on a rock." Rosalind looked at him pleadingly. He had been so kind the night before, not asking any questions when Cagney delivered his oldest daughter, half drowned and with a nasty bruise on her forehead. Was he going to want confessions this morning? She had already confessed it all to herself, tossing and turning on her bed all night. How she'd been a fool, giving her heart to someone who thought of her as a little kid. How she would wait years and years before even thinking about a boy again. Her family, her friends, school—those would be her only concerns from now on.

"But why were Cagney and that girl—"

"Kathleen."

"Ah, yes, Kathleen. Why were they there to rescue you? A mere coincidence?"

"Sort of. I mean, yes."

"And it had nothing to do with the fact that Skye came home dripping wet earlier yesterday? Is Jane next? Will each of my daughters be delivered to me, one at a time, as from the briny deep?"

"Oh, Daddy."

Mr. Penderwick looked around the kitchen as if for help. "Rosalind, you're getting older now. There are things about young women that I simply don't understand. If only your mother—" He stopped. Rosalind's eyes filled with tears. This was worse than confessions. Mr. Penderwick turned back to her. "Tell me this, Rosy. If your mother were alive, would there be anything about last night too shameful to explain to her?"

"No," said Rosalind positively.

"Then I won't worry," said Mr. Penderwick.

"Embarrassing, maybe, but not shameful."

"Don't confuse me."

Skye burst into the room. "Has Jeffrey shown up yet?"

"No," said Rosalind.

"Wow." Skye recoiled at the sight of Rosalind. "What happened to your head?"

"Nothing."

"What do you mean, nothing? That looks even worse than the bonk I gave Jeffrey when I first met him."

"Nothing means she doesn't want to talk about it," said Mr. Penderwick.

Next came Jane. She was dancing and waving a blue notebook in the air. "I've done it! I finished my book! I woke up this morning and the whole ending was right there in my brain—I just had to write it down. Daddy, may I type it on your computer today?"

"Slow down a minute. How do you feel?" said Mr. Penderwick.

"I feel fine, just a little sniffy." Jane illustrated by sniffing loudly. "Finishing my book healed me."

"In that case, certainly you may use my computer. Then will we be allowed to read this masterpiece?"

"Of course, Daddy," said Jane. "Rosalind! Where did you get that bruise?"

"She's not telling," said Skye.

"Why not?"

"Because she chooses not to," said Mr. Penderwick. The telephone rang. Rosalind dove across the kitchen to where it hung on the wall and picked up the receiver. "Hello? Oh, hi, Churchie. Yes, she's here." She turned to Skye and said, "Churchie has a message for you."

"It has to be from Jeffrey." Skye eagerly grabbed the phone.

She was no longer eager, however, when she hung up.

"What happened?" said Rosalind, appalled at the misery on Skye's face.

"Mrs. Tifton and Dexter took Jeffrey to Pennsylvania yesterday," she said.

"Pennsylvania!" cried Jane. "That means Pencey Military Academy!"

"Oh, no." Rosalind dropped into a chair. Her troubles paled in the face of Jeffrey being dragged off to Pencey.

"What fresh mystery is this?" asked Mr. Penderwick.

It took a while to explain everything to him. The three sisters tried to start with Pencey, but to make sense of that, they had to go back and tell about General Framley and West Point. And then, Dexter's loathsome role in everything had to be explained, along with the small bits and pieces they knew about Jeffrey's father. When all of this was done, Skye suddenly blurted out what had happened with Mrs. Tifton the day before in the music room. Or most of it, anyway. She left out what Mrs. Tifton had said about their mother and, to Rosalind's lasting gratitude, what she'd said about Rosalind and Cagney.

"Mrs. Tifton's a mean, awful person," said Jane when Skye had finished.

"And I don't know if Batty's gotten over it yet," said Skye.

Mr. Penderwick looked out the window to where Batty was playing vampires with Hound. Hound was on his back, trying to wiggle out of the black towel Batty had tied around his neck. Batty was leaping over Hound's water bowl, shrieking, "Blood, blood!"

"She looks all right," he said. "But I'll talk to her later."

"But what about Jeffrey?" said Jane. "Do you think they're locking him up in that horrible school right at this actual minute? Will we ever see him again?"

"Churchie didn't know," said Skye. "When they left yesterday afternoon, the only thing Mrs. Tifton said is that she'd be back sometime this afternoon or evening. She only mentioned Pennsylvania at the last minute, and Churchie didn't get a decent chance to talk with Jeffrey. He barely managed to whisper a message before he was dragged off. 'Tell Skye it's not her fault.' That's all he said."

"Churchie must be really upset," said Rosalind.

"Poor Churchie. Poor Jeffrey," said Jane.

"You're all certain Jeffrey doesn't want to go to Pencey?" said Mr. Penderwick. "And that he has no interest in a military career?"

"We're positive," said Skye.

"And he's explained this to his mother? For parents almost always want what's best for their children. They just don't always know what that is."

"He's tried to explain, but she won't listen," said Rosalind.

"That's not good." Mr. Penderwick looked around at the girls. "I hope I always listen. I do try."

"Daddy, don't be silly!" Jane threw herself at him from one side while Rosalind hugged him from the other.

"Well," said Skye. "There was that time you and Mommy made us be flower girls in Uncle Gordon's wedding even though I said over and over I didn't want to."

"Skye, that was six years ago," said Rosalind.

Skye plowed on. "And I had to wear a pink frilly dress and that stupid hat with bows all over it."

"I loved that hat!" said Jane.

"And all the grown-ups kept leaning down and telling me how cute I was." Now Skye was finished.

"I do apologize, Skye. That must have been difficult," said Mr. Penderwick. "I promise I'll never ask you to be a flower girl again."

"Thank you." Skye said it with great dignity.

"But we're too old—" protested Jane.

Rosalind interrupted her with a frown and changed the subject. "Back to Jeffrey and Pencey."

"Yes," said Mr. Penderwick, trying not to smile.

"What can we do to help him?" said Skye.

"I don't know if we can help him," said Mr. Penderwick. "Right now all we can do is wait until he gets back from Pennsylvania."

"If he gets back," said Rosalind.

"Oh!" said Jane.

And depression settled over the kitchen like a wet fog.

Guilt was not a familiar emotion to Skye, but she was feeling it today. Jeffrey could leave a thousand messages about all this not being her fault, and she still wouldn't believe it. If only she hadn't been wrestling with Jeffrey in the music room—if only she hadn't yelled at Mrs. Tifton—if only she weren't such a hot-headed loudmouth—

She was lurking in the Arundel gardens, peering around the edge of a rose arbor, just as she'd been for the last hour or so. During that time, nothing at all had happened. Mrs. Tifton's car was still gone. No one had returned from Pennsylvania. Even Cagney seemed to be nowhere. It was like the place was under a terrible spell, like in dopey *Sleeping Beauty*, she thought, or dopier *Snow White*, or one of those other fairy tales Jane knew by heart.

She'd brought along her math book, and now she plunked down on the bench at the back of the rose arbor and opened it. Maybe working on problems with two variables would distract her. *If a 14-foot piece of wood is cut into two pieces in a ratio of 3 to 4, how long is each piece?*

"Make one piece x and the other y," she said while

210

she scribbled. "So x plus y equals 14. And the proportion is hmmm, hmm, and cross-multiply, then—aha!—substitute. Now $4x$ equals 3 times 14 minus x. x equals 6 and y equals 8. Big deal."

Skye skipped several questions to find something harder, but the math book didn't seem to hold its usual charm. This was the most frustrating day she had ever lived through, and it wasn't even dark yet. Besides the bad news about Jeffrey, her sisters had deserted her. Rosalind was hiding in her bedroom writing a letter to Anna—was she explaining to Anna about that bruise?—and Jane was taking all day to type her Sabrina Starr book into the computer. Even Batty wasn't interested in doing anything. Not that Skye had wanted Batty's company, of course. It wasn't like they'd actually become friends during that walk home in the rain or anything.

So Skye had spent the morning shooting arrows at the Dexter target, but how much fun was that when there was no one to compete with? And then, after lunch, she'd kicked the soccer ball around, but soccer was even worse than archery for doing alone. Finally when she couldn't stand it anymore, she'd come over here and hidden in the rose arbor nearest the driveway. If she was going to be bored and lonely, she might as well watch for Jeffrey at the same time.

Except that now all of a sudden her stomach was rumbling ferociously. She'd long since devoured the

211

tomato-and-cheese sandwich she had brought for provisions, and there was nothing more to eat. Great. Now not only was she bored and lonely—and feeling guilty!—she was hungry.

"Sabrina Starr reporting for duty." Jane's head popped around the side of the rose arbor.

"I thought you were typing," said Skye, trying not to look as relieved as she felt.

"I finished, and Daddy read it. He said it was very good, better even than *Sabrina Starr Rescues a Groundhog*," said Jane. "And then we ate dinner. Daddy sent me to give you a food break, and he says to tell you it's spaghetti, in case you argued with me."

"Why does everybody think I argue? I never argue." Skye hesitated. "Or at least, I'm not going to argue as much anymore."

"That would be a miracle."

Skye chose to pretend she hadn't heard. "Now, Jane, your mission is just to watch and gather information. If they come home, wait until they're inside, then run right back to the cottage to tell us whether or not they brought Jeffrey with them."

"I know all that," said Jane.

"You're sure? You'll remember not to let any grown-ups see you?"

"Skye!"

"All right. I'll be back after I eat." She picked up the math book and zoomed off toward the tunnel.

Jane settled down on the bench and prepared herself for a long wait. She had brought along a box of tissues for her lingering sniffles plus two books. One was *Magic by the Lake*. She'd just gotten to the part where Katharine was stuck in the oil jar in Ali Baba's cave, and although this was the fourth time Jane had read the book, she was excited to read what came next. This is what made a book great, she thought, that you could read it over and over and never get tired of it.

But as much as Jane wanted to read about the genie showing up to get Katharine out of the oil jar, the second book she had brought along—thirty neatly typed pages in a red binder—interested her more. Jane stroked its cover and wondered if anyone would read this book more than once. Or if anyone other than her father would ever read it at all. But no, it was too bad to think that a book could be written with such sweat and joy, then be left to lie alone on a shelf. You deserve attention, dear book, thought Jane, and, with great ceremony, opened the red cover and read the title page:

SABRINA STARR RESCUES A BOY
by Jane Letitia Penderwick

"That looks wonderful." She turned to the next page and started to read. "Chapter one. The lonely boy named Arthur stared sadly out the window, never dreaming that help was on the way. Unknown to him, the great Sabrina Starr—"

Jane paused. A car was coming. She peeked through the roses. It was Mrs. Tifton's! Now Jane would have some news about Jeffrey. Would he be in the car? Or had they left him behind in Pennsylvania?

The car came to a stop. Jane tried to count the number of people inside, but the evening sun was shining on the windows, and even squinting, she couldn't see a thing. The driver's door opened, and out climbed Dexter. He walked around to the passenger's side and opened that door. Mrs. Tifton emerged, wearing a blue dress that matched her car. The two of them turned toward the house, and in that moment Jane was plunged into despair. They had left Jeffrey behind at Pencey. He was even now having his head shaved, locked in a dormitory with a hundred boys who didn't care anything about music.

Then the back door opened, and out came Jeffrey. Jane silently applauded and wiped her imagination clean of Pencey nightmares. Thank goodness he was back. But how was he? Jane couldn't see his face to tell—his camouflage hat was pulled down too low. Well, at least he wasn't wearing one of those dreadful military uniforms yet. There was still hope. Maybe Pencey had rejected him.

Jane watched as Jeffrey trailed Mrs. Tifton and Dexter into the house. She gathered up her books and got ready to run back to the cottage with the news. She would wait two minutes until the coast was clear. She counted the seconds. One, one thousand. Two, one thousand. Three, one thousand. The door opened again, and Dexter came back outside and opened the trunk. Oh, the luggage, thought Jane, and knew that she should wait another moment until Dexter was gone.

If only she *had* waited, sitting quietly on the bench and reading *Magic by the Lake*. But optimistic Jane still clung to her theory that Dexter might have a good side, though she'd been careful never to mention this to her sisters or Jeffrey. For deep down, she knew they would explode the theory and, with it, her hope that the good Dexter—Mr. Dupree—would help with her book.

Jane picked up *Sabrina Starr Rescues a Boy* and clutched it to her heart. There he was, Mr. Dupree the publisher, just thirty feet away. Should she call out to him? Skye had told her not to let the grown-ups see her. But what if he published her book and sold the movie rights, and Jane made enough money to build Skye her own science laboratory in the basement at home? Would that make up for wrecking the mission? What to do? What to do? Dexter was closing the trunk. In a few seconds, she would have missed her opportunity. But what if—? But what if not—? Jane's mind whirled. She couldn't decide.

Her nose decided for her. For just as Dexter picked up the suitcases and started toward the house, a monster tickle attacked her right nostril. She ducked back into the rose arbor, gasped, held her breath, stuffed her hand over her mouth, but it was no good. She exploded with a gigantic sneeze, big enough—she told Skye later—to blow down a dozen rose arbors. And certainly big enough to catch Dexter's attention.

He turned around and yelled, "Who's there?"

This was it, thought Jane. The fates had decided. Gathering up all her courage—and a tissue in case she had to sneeze again—Jane marched out of the rose arbor and across the driveway and said, "Hello, Mr. Dupree. It's me, Jane Penderwick. I brought you my book."

He didn't look happy to see her. "What book?"

Jane held up her precious red binder. "The book I wrote. You said you'd look at it when it was done and give me some pointers."

"You Penderwick kids are unbelievable. This is a joke, right?"

"No, it's not a joke," said Jane, her heart sinking into her shoes. Where, oh where, was nice Mr. Dupree? "I've been working so hard."

Dexter dropped the suitcases and took the red binder from Jane. "I'll take a look at it, but then you have to leave before Brenda catches you trespassing again and has a stroke."

Jane held her breath. This was it. Her whole future was about to be decided. Dexter glanced at the first page of chapter one, flipped to the middle of the book and skimmed another page, then slapped it shut and handed it back to Jane. "You spelled *helium* wrong."

"But what about the story? What about my writing?" gasped Jane.

"What did you expect me to say? It's lousy. Now go away." He picked up the suitcases and strode into the house.

Jane tore page eight out of the red binder, shredded it into little bits, and tossed them onto the floor of her bedroom, where they joined hundreds of other little bits of paper. She tore out page nine and did the same.

"Hello, Jane, are you in there?" It was Skye, knocking on the door.

"Go away," said Jane.

"What's wrong?"

"Nothing." Jane tore out page ten and shredded it.

"Rosalind told me that you saw Jeffrey. We've got a plan, but I can't shout it at you from here."

Jane got up from the bed, went to the door, and opened it a crack. "Tell me."

"You and I are going over to the mansion later to climb the rope ladder and talk to Jeffrey. Rosalind will stay here and cover for us. I'll come get you after Daddy goes to sleep."

"Okay," said Jane.

"Why can't I come in?"

"Because I said so," said Jane, and closed the door. She sat down on the bed again and tore out page eleven.

When she had gotten to page twenty, there was another knock on the door. "Jane?" It was Mr. Penderwick.

"Please go away, Daddy. I want to be alone right now."

"I'm worried about you."

"I'm fine."

"I do have one important question, but I can ask it from out here," said Mr. Penderwick. "Are you dry?"

Jane got off the bed and opened the door so that he could see her. "Of course I'm dry. Why did you ask that?"

"So many daughters have come home wet lately." He looked past her at the paper all over the floor. "What are you doing?"

"If you must know, I'm destroying *Sabrina Starr Rescues a Boy* and then I'm quitting writing. I'm no good and it's time I faced up to it."

"Why, Jane, that's simply not true. You're a superb writer and your new book is a tour de force. That scene where Arthur threw the bread and water back at Ms. Horriferous and said, 'Give me liberty or give me death'? *Excellens, praestans.*"

"You're just saying that because you're my father. Professional people know better."

"What professional people?"

"Dexter, and he's an actual publisher. I showed him

218

my new book, and he told me the truth. He said it was lousy." Jane ripped out another page.

"But my sweet, mad daughter, Dexter doesn't publish books. He publishes a magazine about cars."

Jane stopped tearing. "Cars?"

"It's called *Lines on the Road,* of all things. For all we know, he knows as much about real books as Hound does."

"Are you making this up to make me feel better?"

"Of course not. Cagney told me last week while he was showing me how to propagate *Anemone hupehensis.*"

"Oh, Daddy," said Jane, looking around at the scraps of paper on the floor.

"That wasn't your only copy, was it?"

"It's still on your computer. I was going to erase it tomorrow."

"Well, instead, let's print it out again and keep it forever."

"Are you sure? You really like the scene where Ms. Horriferous shakes her fist out the window at the hot-air balloon?"

"Yes, I loved it."

"And when Sabrina made an emergency landing in Kansas during a tornado?"

"It was perfect."

Jane gazed yearningly up at him. "You're absolutely positive I'm a good writer?"

"Good?" Mr. Penderwick took her face in his hands. "Jane-o, you're much better than good. You have a rare and marvelous gift for words. And your imagination! Do you remember what your mother used to say?"

"That my imagination is the eighth wonder of the world."

"And your mother was a wise woman, wasn't she?"

"Yes, Daddy. I love you."

"I love you, too, daughter. Now clean up this mess and go to bed. Great authors need their rest." And he went out, quietly closing the door behind him.

CHAPTER SIXTEEN
The Runaway

Sᴋʏᴇ ᴡᴀs ʟʏɪɴɢ ᴏɴ ʜᴇʀ ᴛᴜᴇsᴅᴀʏ-Thursday-Saturday bed, listening to the opera music coming through the floor from her father's room, right below hers. A man was singing—in Italian, Skye thought—and he sounded awfully sad.

"*. . . come sei pallida! e stanca, e muta, e bella . . .*"

Skye wasn't crazy about opera. All that screeching and why people couldn't sing in English was beyond her. But her mother had loved it. Daddy must be thinking about her, Skye thought, and wished for the tenth time she'd socked Mrs. Tifton in the nose when she had the chance. Anyone who could say those things about Elizabeth Penderwick deserved a broken nose. Then Skye reminded herself—also for the tenth time—that she shouldn't be fantasizing about socking Mrs. Tifton. Yelling at her had been bad enough. She sat up and swung her arms around wildly. This controlling her temper wasn't going to be easy.

The music stopped. A few more minutes and her father would go to sleep, and then she and Jane could finally go see Jeffrey. Skye got off the bed and looked out the window. There was plenty of moonlight—she and Jane wouldn't have any trouble climbing the rope ladder tonight.

But what was that? Someone or something was moving through the trees. Was it Hound? No, Hound was asleep in Batty's room. Skye strained to see through the shadows. There it was again! It looked like a person, but with an odd shape. A hunchback? Who was it? And now he was lifting something up. *Thwonk!* A rubber-tipped arrow hit the screen right in front of her face.

"Jeffrey?" she called softly.

Jeffrey stepped out into the moonlight. He was wearing his camouflage hat and a backpack and was carrying a bow. "Let me in."

"I'll be right down." Skye ran out of her room and down the hall to Rosalind's room.

Rosalind peeked out. "Ready to go?"

"Change of plans. Emergency MOOPS. Your room. Back in a minute," Skye whispered, then went quietly down the steps and out the front door. "What are you doing here? We were just about to come see you."

"I'm running away." Jeffrey put down the bow.

"Are you nuts?"

"If you'd seen Pencey—"

"Oh, Jeffrey." Skye felt like crying, which never happened to her. "This is all my fault. I should never have said those things to your mother."

"Didn't Churchie give you my message? It wasn't your fault. Besides—" He looked down at the ground and shuffled his feet. "You stood up for yourself. You have courage."

"It's not courage. It's just temper."

He looked up again. "It *is* courage, but let's not argue. I want to tell you and your sisters what happened in Pennsylvania and where I'm going. Can I come in?"

Skye took his hand, and together they crept back into the house and up the stairs to Rosalind's room. Rosalind and Jane were sitting on the bed, waiting for the MOOPS to begin. They weren't expecting Skye to have someone with her.

"Jeffrey!" said Rosalind.

"He's running away," said Skye.

"Oh, dear, oh, dear," said Jane. "Jeffrey, are you sure?"

"Yes, I'm sure. Pencey—"

"Wait a minute, Jeffrey," said Rosalind. "We'd better

make this official, just in case you tell us anything we have to keep secret. Do you mind waiting out in the hall for a minute?"

"He doesn't have to. He already knows about Penderwick Family Honor," said Jane. "We told him after he rescued Batty from the—"

"Rosebush," said Skye.

"All those thorns," said Jane.

"All right," said Rosalind, looking from one fibber to the other. "Then let's get started. MOOPS come to order."

The closet door swung open and out sprang Hound, his tail wagging furiously. He jumped on Jeffrey and licked his face. Next through came Batty in her pajamas, holding Funty.

"You woke up Hound," she said. "Hi, Jeffrey."

"Hi, Batty. Where are your wings?"

"I take them off to sleep, silly."

"Batty, go back to bed," said Skye.

"No," she said, cuddling up next to Rosalind.

"I'd like her to stay, if it's all right," said Jeffrey.

"Batty, you have to be really, really quiet," said Rosalind. "You too, Hound."

Hound flopped onto the floor with a grunt. Jeffrey took off his backpack and settled down next to Hound.

"Ready, everyone?" said Rosalind. "Emergency MOOPS—no, MOPS—come to order."

"Second the motion," said Skye.

"Third it," said Jane.

"Fourth," said Batty.

"All swear to keep secret what is said here, even from Daddy, unless you think someone might do something truly bad," said Rosalind, and held out her fist. Skye put her fist on top of Rosalind's, Jane put hers on top of Skye's, and Batty put hers on top of Jane's.

"You too," said Rosalind to Jeffrey, and he put his fist on top of Batty's.

"This I swear, by the Penderwick Family Honor," they all said, then broke their fists apart.

"Now, Jeffrey, tell us everything from the beginning," said Rosalind.

"It started yesterday, when Mother was furious at me because—" He looked at Skye.

"I told them," she said.

"Well, because of what happened in the music room. She was so angry she could barely talk to me. She just sent me to my room and told me to wait there. So I started playing the piano and the next thing I know Mother's barging in, telling me to pack an overnight bag and that I should include a suit and tie because we were going to Pencey for an interview. An interview—just like that, all of a sudden! I got really upset and tried to tell her about not wanting to go to Pencey, but she wouldn't listen. She just said that I'd brought all this on myself and told me to hurry up with the packing. And then she ordered me downstairs and into Dexter's car, and we all started driving toward Pennsylvania."

The sisters shivered. For the rest of their lives, they would want nothing to do with that state.

"When we got there, we stayed in a hotel, and that was sort of okay because I had my own room and there was this great old black-and-white movie on television called *To Kill a Mockingbird*." Jeffrey stopped and looked like he was remembering the movie. "Anyway, the next morning they took me to Pencey. It was even more horrible than I'd thought it would be. Everyone was frowning and saluting and marching around with rifles. I had an interview with Major Somebody who served under my grandfather in Vietnam and all he could talk about was how my grandfather was his idol. When he asked me why I wanted to go to Pencey, I told him it was the last place in the world I wanted to go, and he just laughed and patted me on the shoulder and said I'd feel different after I'd lived like a real soldier for a few weeks.

"After that, we went out to lunch—Dexter, Mother, and me—and they told me I'd be starting at Pencey in three weeks. Old Dexter tried to make it sound all terrific—he kept saying how grateful I should be that my mother wanted to send me to such a good school. When he finally shut up, I tried to tell Mother how much I hated Pencey and how going there would make me miserable, but she just cut me off again and said that a little discipline never harmed anyone, especially boys who'd been associating with the wrong kind of people—sorry, I should have left that part out."

"Don't worry about it," said Rosalind.

"I'm proud to be the wrong kind of people," said Jane.

"Me too," said Batty. "So's Hound."

"What happened next?" said Skye.

"We drove back home, with Dexter going on and on about all the rich families that send their sons to Pencey and how there's this golf course across the street from the school and I'll be able to use my spare time playing golf, and Mother agreeing with him and saying how she was sure I'd love it when I got settled in. I didn't say a word—not a word—the whole ride home. I just sat in the backseat and planned how I was going to run away." Jeffrey rubbed his eyes, hard, then started talking again very quickly. "And that's what I did. I went up to my room, pretending like everything was okay, and got ready to leave. I put their golf bag under the covers of my bed so that if Mother looks in, she'll think I'm asleep. Then I climbed down the rope ladder and came over here to say good-bye. I'll sleep tonight under Harry's tomato stand. When Harry shows up in the morning, I'll ask him to drive me to the bus station."

Skye broke in. "But where are you going?"

"Boston. Churchie's daughter lives there, and she'll let me stay with her for a while, I know she will. I'll go to public school, and I'll get a job teaching little kids to play the piano so that I can pay for classes at that New England Conservatory of Music I told you about. Don't laugh."

"We're not laughing," said Rosalind.

"Because it's not as crazy as it sounds. If Churchie's daughter can't keep me, I have some distant cousins in Boston that Mother hasn't spoken to in years. Maybe when they find out she's not speaking to me, either, they'll like me and take me in until I'm a little older. I've got my birthday money still, which will pay for the bus ticket. Plus I've got these." Jeffrey opened his backpack, pulled out several slim leather-bound books, and opened one. It was filled with unfamiliar-looking coins. "My grandfather collected rare coins and gave them to me before he died. I think they're worth a lot. I should be able to sell them in Boston. Right?"

"Right," said Jane.

"And besides, maybe I'll find my—" He stopped, all of a sudden very busy petting Hound's ears.

"Your what?" asked Batty.

For a long while, there was no sound in the room except Hound's happy panting.

"I think he means his father," said Skye finally.

Jeffrey stared defiantly around the circle of sisters. "Mother first met him in Boston, you know. He might still be there. And it's true that I don't know his last name, but I don't look anything like Mother or Grandfather, either, no matter what Mother says, so I must look like my father—and then maybe I'll pass him on the street one day and he'll recognize me and I'll recognize him. It's not impossible!"

"Of course not," said Jane. "The gods of fate may be kind."

Jeffrey gave her a grateful smile. "That's what I thought."

"Well—" said Rosalind.

"And I'll go with you to keep you company until Boston," said Jane. "Then I can get a bus back to Cameron and meet Daddy and everybody day after tomorrow, when they go home."

"What?" cried Skye. "I'm older! If anybody goes, it's me."

"Order!" said Rosalind.

"I called dibs on it," said Jane.

"Can I go, too?" said Batty.

"Order, come to order!" Rosalind pounded her fist into the bed.

"But—" said Skye.

"Be quiet, Skye. I'm serious," said Rosalind. "We have to talk about this calmly. First of all, Jeffrey, you know your mother will come after you. If she can't find you right away, she'll send the police."

"I don't care," he said. "I won't go to Pencey. And I won't live with Dexter, either. Mother can do whatever she wants. I won't change my mind. And what does it matter to her and Dexter where I am, anyway? They just want to get rid of me."

"I don't know what the laws are, but—"

"This isn't about law, Rosy," said Jane. "This is about heart and truth and adventure."

"And sticking up for yourself," said Skye.

"I see all that, and I know Jeffrey's mother isn't very good at listening"—Skye tried to interrupt, but Rosalind silenced her with a stern look—"but, Jeffrey, she does want what's best for you, even if she doesn't know what that is. If there's some way to make her understand how you feel about Pencey—"

"I can't make her understand!" Jeffrey cried it out like he was in pain. "I've tried and tried and tried."

"I know you have." And Rosalind did know. She knew he'd tried as much as anyone could expect him to.

"I've got to go, Rosalind, don't you see?"

Against her better judgment, Rosalind told the truth. "Yes, I do see."

"Hurray!" said Jane.

"Thank you, Rosalind," said Jeffrey. He suddenly looked desperately tired.

"But!" Rosalind held up her hand for order. "None of us are going along with him to Boston. How could you even think of doing that to Daddy?"

"You're right," said Jane. "But we'll visit Jeffrey after he's settled."

"And he can visit us in Cameron," said Skye.

"To see Hound," said Batty.

"Definitely. Oh, and that reminds me. I brought something for Batty." Jeffrey reached into his back-pack and pulled out the picture of Hound she had given him for his birthday. "You keep this for me until I see you again, okay?"

"Okay." Batty took the picture and showed it to Hound.

"All right, then," said Rosalind. "Now, Jeffrey, there's no need for you to sleep under Harry's stand tonight. Batty can sleep in here with me, and you can have her room. I'll set my alarm clock and get you up and out of here early."

"Wake us up, too, so we can say good-bye," said Skye.

"And put together provisions for the hungry traveler," said Jane.

"Now everyone go to bed," said Rosalind. "It's late."

Jane and Skye went off to their rooms, and Jeffrey took his backpack into Batty's room and stretched out on the bed in his clothes, but Batty had a lot of organizing to do before she could go to sleep. She had to tuck Funty into Rosalind's bed, then go back through the closet for Ursula the bear and then again for Fred the other bear. Rosalind put her foot down about Sedgewick the horse and Yaz, the new wooden rabbit—she said there would be no room left for people. Then Batty decided she couldn't sleep without her special unicorn blanket, so Jeffrey had to get up and let Rosalind switch that blanket with the green blanket from Rosalind's bed.

Batty finally agreed to settle down, but then there was the problem of Hound. What with Jeffrey in Batty's bed and Batty in Rosalind's bed with Rosalind, he was very confused. Where was he supposed to sleep? He knew Rosalind wouldn't allow him on her bed, even if there had been room. On the other hand, he knew that Jeffrey would allow him on his bed and he did love Jeffrey madly, but Jeffrey wasn't Batty. What was a dog to do? He went back and forth through the closet several times, whining, until Rosalind closed both doors and ordered him to sleep on the floor beside her bed.

"Guard Batty," she said, which wasn't quite fair, because Batty didn't need guarding. But at least it was something that Hound understood. He gave out a great doggy sigh of relief, collapsed onto the floor, and fell instantly asleep.

Batty, too, was asleep in minutes. Then it was just Rosalind lying awake, worried about Jeffrey and whether she should be letting him run away. If he hadn't talked about his father like that—oh! the hungry look on his face—maybe she would have tried harder to talk him into staying. But still, was she making a terrible mistake? She wished she had someone to talk it over with, someone other than her younger sisters, who thought everything in life was an adventure. Someone like Cagney, for example. Except that she would never be able to talk comfortably with Cagney again. She might never talk to him again, period. He'd dropped by earlier to check on her, but she'd hidden like a baby in her bedroom, and now they were going home to Cameron the day after next, and he probably wouldn't try again. She would have nothing but memories, for she'd thrown away the white rose from his Fimbriata bush and asked her father to give back the Gettysburg book.

Memories and her bruise. She wriggled her arm out from under the covers and probed the sore place on her head. It was still painful—her father said it would be for a while—but at least it didn't show anymore for she'd rearranged her hair to cover it. Not much of a memento. Oh, well. She didn't really care about Cagney, him and his pretty Kathleen. Rosalind gave out a great sigh that sounded like Hound's, but hers wasn't of relief. Then at long last, blessedly, she fell asleep.

CHAPTER SEVENTEEN
The Next-to-Last Day

Batty woke up before Rosalind's alarm clock went off. There's no need for an alarm when a dog is licking your face.

"Go away," she whispered to Hound. He pranced across the room and whined at the closet door. That wouldn't do—he would wake up Rosalind, who was still dreaming next to Ursula the bear. Batty slid out from bed, grabbed Hound by the collar, and tugged. Hound sat down and refused to budge. She tugged harder. All in vain.

Disgusted, Batty let go of Hound, padded over to the bedroom door, and opened it. Almost before she could leave the room, Hound had bounded past her and down the hall to plant himself in front of her bedroom door. "You want to see Jeffrey, don't you?" she said.

Hound looked mournfully at her. "Well, I'd like to see him, too. But we can't, 'cause he's still asleep. So there." Hound answered with one short, defiant yip, but when Batty started down the steps to the kitchen, he followed her.

Cereal was the only kind of breakfast Batty was allowed to fix by herself, and since the day she had spilled a gallon of milk on Hound's head, it had to be cereal without milk. She pulled a chair over to the counter, climbed on it, got down the Cheerios box, and climbed off the chair. Just as she did every morning, she first poured Cheerios onto the floor for Hound to lick up, then let him out the back door for what Mr. Penderwick called his morning rituals.

Now it was time for her own meal. She took the Peter Pan bowl off the low shelf where it was kept for her and paused with the Cheerios box in midair. Outside, Hound was barking as though under attack by aliens from outer space. Batty looked out the screen door. It wasn't aliens, though they would have seemed scarcely less dreadful to Batty. It was Mrs. Tifton and Dexter, and Hound was doing his best to keep them away from the cottage. Batty backed away from the door, but she was too late—Mrs. Tifton had seen her.

"Bitty! Let us in," she heard Mrs. Tifton yell.

"Good dog." That was Dexter, and Batty could tell he didn't mean it.

Mrs. Tifton was shouting again. "Dexter, get that dog out of my way!"

To Batty's horror, the next thing she heard was a smack and a loud dog yelp. She threw open the screen door and cried out to Hound. He rushed in and Batty threw her arms around his neck and whispered soothing love words in his ear.

Now Mrs. Tifton and Dexter were right at the door, peering in at Batty. Mrs. Tifton wasn't her usual tidy self. Her hair was sticking up in strange places, and she was wearing bedroom slippers and an old raincoat over her nightgown.

"Bitty, we're looking for Jeffrey. May we come in?" she said.

Batty's answer was to lock the screen door.

"By God, she's locked us out, Dexter!" said Mrs. Tifton. "Where's your father, you naughty child?"

"Remember, Brenda, she doesn't talk," said Dexter.

"I heard her call the dog. She can talk if she wants to. Tell us if Jeffrey's here! I want my son!"

Batty wanted to run away from these awful people. But then who would stop them from coming into the house and hitting Hound again and finding Jeffrey and dragging him away? She had to be strong. Skye had said she was perfect. Well then, she would be perfect and protect the dog and people she loved.

Batty drew herself up and faced the enemy boldly. "It's

not that I can't talk. It's that I don't like you, and Daddy says we're allowed to choose the people we talk to."

"Your daddy can go to—" spat Mrs. Tifton.

"Brenda, please," said Dexter. "Let me handle this."

"Handle what?" said a voice behind Batty. "Good morning, Batty."

"Oh, Daddy!" Batty threw her arms around his knees. "They hit Hound."

"The child's exaggerating," said Dexter. "I gave the dog a gentle tap to stop his barking. Pardon me, this hasn't been the best introduction. I'm Dexter Dupree. You're Martin Penderwick?"

"Glad to meet you, and good morning, Mrs. Tifton," said Mr. Penderwick, stroking Batty's curls. "What can I do for you?"

"It's Jeffrey. He's gone. I woke up early because I was worried. You see, we'd gone on a trip and had a terrible argument—"

"Not terrible," said Dexter.

"—and I went to see if he was feeling better and he wasn't in his room. There was only a golf bag in his bed and this note." She pressed a scrap of paper against the screen.

"I'll never go to Pencey. Don't bother to look for me," read Mr. Penderwick.

"I don't understand the boy. Pencey is an excellent school," said Dexter.

"Shut up, Dexter," said Mrs. Tifton.

"That's dreadful news," said Mr. Penderwick. "But why have you come to us? Jeffrey hasn't been here since the day before yesterday."

"Oh my God." Mrs. Tifton swayed a little. "I was hoping I'd find him here. Your daughters, though, they'll know where he's gone. Please ask your daughters."

"Batty, do you know where Jeffrey is?" asked Mr. Penderwick, looking down at her. She said not a word but looked up at him pleadingly, with all her heart in her face. After a long moment, Mr. Penderwick unlocked the screen door. "I think you two had better come inside and sit down for a few minutes. I'll go upstairs and speak with the older three."

"I'll come with you," said Mrs. Tifton, bursting into the house and heading for the stairs.

"It's best for you to wait down here," said Mr. Penderwick.

"I—" she said.

"Sit, please," said Mr. Penderwick, firmly but kindly.

Mrs. Tifton collapsed into a kitchen chair and buried her face in her hands. Dexter, whose shoes Hound was suspiciously sniffing, sat down next to her and lifted his feet in the air.

"Come, Hound. You too, Batty," said Mr. Penderwick, and the three of them climbed the stairs. Mr. Penderwick knocked on Rosalind's door.

The door opened a crack and Rosalind peeked out. "Good morning, Daddy. Whoops," she said, and dove away from the door to turn off the alarm clock, which had just started beeping. As soon as she let go of the door, Hound pushed through, ran over to her closet, and barked. Rosalind grabbed him and dragged him back into the hall. As soon as she let go, he sidled down to Batty's door and barked again.

"What's wrong with Hound?" asked Mr. Penderwick.

"Nothing," said Batty.

By now, the noise had woken Skye and Jane, and they had joined the crowd in the hall.

"What's happening?" said Jane, still half asleep. "Is Jeff—"

Skye kicked her.

"Hound, be quiet!" said Mr. Penderwick. Hound flopped down and started licking Batty's door. "Now, girls."

"Yes, Daddy," answered all four, each looking impossibly innocent.

"Mrs. Tifton and Mr. Dupree are downstairs. They seem to have lost Jeffrey. I'm trusting that Jane hasn't carried him off in a hot-air balloon."

"Oh, Daddy, of course not," said Jane.

"That's a good start. Now, to proceed a little further, can any of you tell me where he is?" No one answered. "Rosalind?"

"No, Daddy, we may not," said Rosalind. Oh, if

only she'd let Jeffrey sleep under Harry's tomato stand! He'd be long gone by now.

"May you tell me if he's safe?" he asked, scanning their faces carefully.

"Yes, he's safe," said Rosalind.

"And comfortable?"

"Yes."

"Is he in Batty's room?"

There was a terrible silence, and everyone hung their heads.

"Oh, daughters," said Mr. Penderwick.

"If you knew everything, you'd understand," said Skye.

"Please don't tell Mrs. Tifton he's here," said Jane.

"I have to tell her something. The poor woman is worried sick." He thought for a minute. "All right. I'll tell her that all I know so far is that he's safe and that I'll call her after I've tortured the whole truth out of my children. In the meantime, if any of you four happen to see Jeffrey"—he stepped closer to Batty's door and raised his voice—"tell him not to worry too much. He's not alone in this."

The door opened slowly and out stepped Jeffrey, very rumpled and with dark circles under his eyes. "Good morning, Mr. Penderwick. I'm sorry to have caused so much trouble."

"No trouble at all, son," said Mr. Penderwick. "Would you like me to tell your mother you're here?"

"Thank you, but I should go down and tell her myself."

"Jeffrey, no!" said Skye. "Let Daddy do it."

"It's over, Skye. I might as well go down there and face up to it," said Jeffrey. "Besides, Rosalind said I should try one more time to get Mother to listen to me about Pencey, and I guess this is my chance."

"But what if I was wrong?" Rosalind clutched her father's arm. She couldn't bear sending Jeffrey downstairs to suffer again.

"You weren't wrong," said Mr. Penderwick. "Jeffrey, would you like me to go with you?"

"Yes, sir." Jeffrey squared his shoulders. "Please."

"We all will," said Rosalind.

"Maybe just Jane." It killed Skye to say this. "She's the only one that Mrs. Tifton doesn't completely despise. But, Jeffrey, the rest of us will be right here if you need anyone to beat anyone else up. Just kidding, Daddy."

"Ha," he said, not without humor, then stepped back so that Jeffrey could lead.

It was a solemn parade downstairs, with Jane at the rear behind Jeffrey and her father. She was proud to be part of Jeffrey's honor guard, but she had hoped never to see that Dexter again. And there he was, lolling sleepily at the kitchen table. What did he care if Jeffrey's whole future was at stake? Creep!

And now Mrs. Tifton was out of her chair, rushing across the room. "Jeffrey, oh, my baby."

242

She hugged him close for a long time, murmuring little words of mother love. Jane's eyes welled with tears, and it was hard work to remember how much she disliked Mrs. Tifton. But then the sweet murmuring stopped, and Mrs. Tifton's sharp voice was back.

"How could you do this to me?"

"I'm sorry, Mother. I didn't mean to upset you."

"Not upset me! What were you thinking?" She held him at arm's length. "That I wouldn't be upset if my only son ran away?"

Jeffrey wriggled free. "I just—"

"Well, you're safe and I suppose that's what's important, though of course there has to be some kind of punishment. But let's go home now and forget about it until we're all thinking more clearly." It was obvious that Mrs. Tifton thought she was being generous.

"No," said Jeffrey.

"No?" she said, her hands on her hips. "What do you mean, no?"

"I want to talk now, before we go home."

"Don't push your luck, young man. I've been amazingly patient so far, considering what you've put me through."

Jeffrey looked over at Mr. Penderwick, who nodded encouragingly. He took a deep breath and tried again. "Mother, I have something very important to tell you. I've tried to tell you before, but you've never listened. Please listen this time. Please."

"This is ridiculous. When don't I listen to you, Jeffrey?"

"Just sit down and let me talk. Please."

"Brenda, honey." Dexter was no longer looking so sleepy. Perhaps he was worried about his own future. "You don't have to do this in front of these people."

Jane bristled. These people, indeed. Someday when she was famous and on television talk shows, she would tell the story of Dexter Dupree, Mr. Lines on the Road, and humiliate him in front of the world.

"Just one minute and then I'll go home. I promise," said Jeffrey.

Mrs. Tifton looked from Dexter to Jeffrey, then sat down in her chair. "It's all right, Dexter. There's nothing Jeffrey can say that could embarrass me. If he has something so important to discuss, I'll listen for a minute. One minute, young man, that's all you have."

"I don't want to go to Pencey. Not next month, not next year, not ever."

Mrs. Tifton stood up. "We're not going over that again."

"Mother, you said you'd listen." She sat down again. "I loved Grandpa. You know I did, and I still miss him. But I'm not him, and I'm not like him."

"Yes, you are, dear. This is silly. We've known ever since you were a baby—"

"You've known, and Grandpa knew. But you never asked me what I thought."

244

"Why, you used to march around wearing that little military cap that Papa gave you for Christmas and call yourself General Jeffrey, and you looked so happy."

"I don't remember any of that."

"You were very young then. Two or three, I suppose." She stopped, confused.

Jeffrey moved closer to his mother. "Do *you* remember telling me about when Grandpa tried to teach you how to swim?"

"Of course I do." Mrs. Tifton shifted uncomfortably in her chair.

"You were five years old and you were terrified of the water, but he insisted you learn, and you begged and begged, until Grandpa just picked you up and threw you into the deep—"

Mrs. Tifton made a little sound at the back of her throat, and Jane saw tears sparkling in her eyes.

Jeffrey paused, uncertain for a moment, then went on. "He threw you into the deep water and you thought you were going to drown and you cried out for help and he just kept shouting SWIM, SWIM, until finally Grandma ran over and pulled you out."

"I don't understand why you're talking about this now," she said, definitely crying now. "I forgave Papa for that long ago. He was just doing what he thought was best for me."

"I know that. But, Mother—" He waited while she

wiped her eyes. "You still don't know how to swim, do you?"

"Oh, Jeffrey, I'm so—I'm so—" She looked wildly around the room. "Dexter! I need to go home! Take me home!"

Dexter was immediately out of his chair, half supporting, half carrying Mrs. Tifton toward the door. Scared and bewildered, Jane tugged on her father's shirt. "Jeffrey didn't finish. Don't let them leave."

"But he made a very good beginning. Go to him."

Jane rushed over to Jeffrey, now all alone in the middle of the kitchen. "Oh, Jeffrey, Jeffrey, you were so fabulously brave."

White and stricken, he looked almost as though he didn't recognize her. "Brave?" he said, then flinched as the door slammed shut behind his mother and Dexter.

"Son, you'd better go with them," said Mr. Penderwick.

"Not yet, Daddy," said Jane.

"Yes, Jane-o, it's best. For now, he must keep talking with his mother."

Jane tore over to the bottom of the stairs and shouted up at her startled sisters, "Quick, he's leaving!"

Seconds later, everyone had dashed downstairs and Skye was pressing Jeffrey's backpack into his arms.

"Are you all right?" she said.

"I don't know."

"It's time, Jeffrey," said Mr. Penderwick. "I'm proud of you."

"Thank you, sir." He threw the backpack over his shoulder and went out the door.

"Jeffrey, we're going home tomorrow morning!" Skye cried after him.

"He knows, sweetheart," said Mr. Penderwick. "We've done all we can. It's between him and his mother now."

Now there was nothing left but to get ready to leave Arundel. They had to organize and pack and clean, all those melancholy end-of-vacation chores that take so much longer than they should. By the time all that was over, it had started to rain again, not the kind of good strong rain that pounds soothingly on the roof and windows, but an annoying drizzle that made everyone feel damp and restless. No one wanted to go out into it, but inside was too depressing with all the packed boxes waiting by the front door. Finally Mr. Penderwick—after much Latin that was probably about daughters and mopiness—came up with the idea of farewell gifts for Jeffrey. So Rosalind made her last batch of Arundel brownies, all for Jeffrey, with none set aside for Cagney. Jane bound another copy of *Sabrina Starr Rescues a Boy* and wrote *To Jeffrey, Love from the Author* on the title page. After a long internal struggle, Batty decided to give back to Jeffrey the photograph of Hound, but as it was already his, it didn't really count, so she also got out her crayons and drew a picture of the bull. Luckily, she wasn't much of an artist, and Rosalind thought the picture was of Hound and even printed HOUND across the top in neat letters. That left only Skye, fretting and fuming to come up with a grand gesture. At last she had an inspiration. She emptied one of the packed boxes—by transferring Batty's stuffed animals to paper bags—cut it apart, and reconstructed it as a flat piece of cardboard. On this she painted a new Dexter target, larger than the old one and with an even smirkier face, and instead of plain D. D. across the bottom, D. D. D. D. for Dreadful Dopey Dexter Dupree. It was a truly impressive target, she thought, and would give Jeffrey an extra special reason to remember her.

And all through that oh-so-long and dreary day, what about Jeffrey? The sisters took turns watching out the window for him, but he never came, and he never called. It made them sick with worry not to know what was happening. They couldn't simply knock on Mrs. Tifton's door and ask—those days were over—and they didn't dare telephone. Finally that evening, when no one could stand it anymore, they voted that Skye sneak over to the rope-ladder tree and climb up to see Jeffrey. But as they had feared, the rope ladder was gone, and though there was a light in Jeffrey's window, Skye returned to the cottage knowing as little as when she had left.

"Were you even sure he was up there?" said Jane.

"Did you see his shadow or hear the piano or anything at all?"

"No," said Skye. "Nothing."

"Dexter could have murdered him and stuffed him in the closet," said Jane. "We'd never know."

"If Dexter hurts a hair on Jeffrey's head, I'll murder *him.*"

"I'll help," said Batty, boldly waving Funty in the air.

"No one's murdering anyone." Rosalind gave Skye and Jane the now-look-what-you've-done frown.

"Sorry," said Jane, twisting and tugging at her curls with frustration. "I just can't stand this waiting."

"We're going home first thing tomorrow," said Skye. "What if Jeffrey hasn't come by then?"

"He'll come," said Rosalind. "He's got to."

CHAPTER EIGHTEEN
Good-bye for Now

BUT THE NEXT MORNING, the car was loaded and the cottage key slid under the mat, and the only person there to say good-bye was Harry, in a black HARRY'S TOMATOES shirt.

"Black because I'm sorry you're leaving," he said. "I'll miss the excitement."

"And you haven't heard any news about Jeffrey?" said Skye.

"You mean since he ran away and his mother found him hiding with you?" Harry shook his head. "I really am going to miss the excitement."

"Harry, tell him we left presents on the front porch," said Jane.

"I'll do that." Harry handed a large paper bag to Mr. Penderwick. "Tomatoes."

"Thanks, Harry. All right, girls, it's time. Pile in."

"A little longer, Daddy," said Jane. "Maybe he'll still come."

"If he hasn't by now, I don't think he will. I'm sorry, honey, but we need to start on our way."

Skye and Jane stuffed Hound into the back with the suitcases and boxes, then everyone slid into their seats, taking the same spots they'd had arriving three weeks earlier. They looked as miserable as it's possible to look without crying, and probably some of them were.

"I didn't say good-bye to Yaz and Carla," said Batty. "They'll be disappointed."

"You can send them a postcard when we get home," said Rosalind.

"And Churchie. Let's send her one, too."

"Good idea."

"And Jeffrey?"

"Oh!" said Jane. She was definitely one of the criers.

"If we haven't heard from Jeffrey in a few days, I'll call and make sure I talk with Churchie, I promise," said Mr. Penderwick. Harry was pulling away in his tomato truck. "Say good-bye to Harry."

"Good-bye, Harry! Thank you for the tomatoes!" The sisters waved out the car windows while Hound barked unhappily in the back.

"Here we go." Mr. Penderwick started the engine

251

and headed down the driveway. Four heads turned to watch the yellow cottage disappear slowly into the trees.

"Good-bye, white bedroom," said Skye.

"Good-bye, secret passage in the closet," said Batty.

"Good-bye, dearest Jeffrey and Churchie and summer and magic and adventure and all that's wonderful in life," said Jane.

Good-bye, Cagney's Fimbriata rosebush, thought Rosalind, and good-bye, Cagney. She turned around and unfolded the map, a brand-new uneaten one. There was the route home, marked in red—she'd done that the night before—but the red line was oddly blurry. Annoyed, Rosalind dashed the tears out of her eyes. At the end of the driveway, we turn right onto Stafford Street, she told herself resolutely, then we go left on—

"Whoops," said Mr. Penderwick, stepping on the brakes.

He'd left his glasses on the kitchen counter and had to run back for them. Which meant that Skye and Jane had the chance to check the tunnel for Jeffrey one last time—and in a flash, they were out of the car and racing off.

Rosalind turned around and looked at Batty, very small and woebegone in the backseat.

"Are you all right?" she asked.

"No."

"Endings are sad, aren't they?"

"Yes." And way in the back, Hound whimpered in agreement.

Rosalind was trying not to whimper herself. For now that it was too late, all of a sudden she knew she'd made a mistake. I'm an idiot, she thought. I'm only twelve years old—well, twelve and a half—and Cagney's much too grown-up to be my boyfriend, but he was my friend and I hid from him the last time he came to see me. And he didn't come to say good-bye today and if he remembers me at all, he'll remember me as this little jerk who fell into the pond and ruined his date and I'll never see him again ever, for the rest of my life. If only, if only—

"Hey, Rosalind."

And there he was at her window, in his Red Sox cap, friendly and cheerful and just the same as always. Rosalind's "if onlys" floated away, and she was left with that now-familiar hit-by-a-truck feeling. And although it was a nice feeling this time, her heart was beating so quickly and her breath was so queerly shallow that she couldn't say anything but could only open the door and stumble out of the car. Cagney caught and steadied her before she fell down altogether.

"Still having trouble with your head?" he asked.

"No—yes—I mean—"

"Let me see."

She pushed aside her hair and let him gravely inspect her bruise while she tried to calm her nerves.

"Doesn't look like there'll be any permanent damage," he said. "Unless you had a concussion and that's why you're babbling."

"I am not babbling." She said it very slowly and precisely.

"Good." He looked into the car. "You've lost most of your family."

"Daddy's getting his glasses from the cottage and Skye and Jane are looking for Jeffrey. They'll all be back soon."

Now Rosalind noticed that Cagney was holding a pet carrier. Glad for an excuse to avoid his gaze, she bent down and peered in at two funny bundles of fur, squished side by side. "You brought the rabbits," she said.

"They're why I'm late," said Cagney. "First Carla hid behind the refrigerator and then Yaz wouldn't let me catch him for the longest time, but I thought Batty might like to see them again before she went home."

Rosalind's heart, whose beating had slowed down a bit, now swelled to twice its normal size with gratitude. She called into the car. "Batty, the bunnies are here to say good-bye!"

"I brought you something, too." Cagney reached

behind him and picked up a large pot. "It's a Fimbriata rose. I figured you deserved one of your own, after helping me with mine."

"Oh, Cagney." Rosalind took the pot and buried her nose in a white bloom. A present. She didn't have a present for him. She should have given him some of those brownies after all. Would she ever understand boys, in her whole entire life? And what should she say now? Then, thank heavens, Batty was out of the car and throwing herself at the pet carrier, and Rosalind was able to figure out her next lines.

"Thank you so much for the Fimbriata. I'll take care of it forever. And thank you for bringing Yaz and Carla. Batty desperately wanted to say good-bye to them." Just as I desperately wanted to say good-bye to you. It was on Rosalind's face, but she didn't say it.

"Well, really it was Yaz's idea." Cagney took a carrot out of his pocket and let Batty feed it to the rabbits.

Over his shoulder, Rosalind could see her father returning, and now she heard Skye and Jane's voices—they were headed back, too. Take courage, Rosy, she thought, this is your last chance to act mature. "And please say good-bye to your—to Kathleen, and thank her for me."

"Who?"

What did he mean, who? "You know, the girl who helped pull me out of the pond."

"Oh, Kathleen, that didn't work out. She wasn't easy to talk to, not like you. Hold on to that skill, Rosy, for when you're old enough to care about boys. They'll appreciate it."

Suddenly he was leaning over her and planting a light kiss on the top of Rosalind's head. Her eyes fluttered closed, and she thought, Finally something wonderful to tell Anna, until she opened her eyes again and saw that he was kissing Batty before strolling away toward Skye and Jane. Probably to kiss them, too! I'll be lucky if he doesn't kiss Daddy and Hound before he's done. Well, at least I'm the only one with a rosebush.

"Why do you look so funny?" said Batty.

"I don't."

"Yes, you do. Like you're going to laugh and cry at the same time."

Rosalind carefully stowed her Fimbriata on the floor of the car, where she'd be able to watch over it during the ride to Cameron. "I'm just glad to be going home, that's all."

A few minutes later, all the Penderwicks were back in the car, once more waving good-bye.

"Good-bye, Cagney," said Mr. Penderwick. "Thanks for all the plant talks."

"Good-bye, Yaz and Carla," said Batty. "I love you."

"Good-bye, Jeffrey, darn-it-all-where-are-you-even-Cagney-doesn't-have-a-clue?" said Skye.

"Good-bye, sanity, because not knowing is driving me crazy," said Jane.

Rosalind waved and smiled one last time to Cagney—farewell!—then smoothed out the map. "Stafford Street, where's Stafford Street," she muttered, then realized she was holding the silly thing upside down. With much rustling, she flipped it and—

"Daddy, stop!" Skye shouted from the backseat. "It's Churchie!"

And there was Churchie, jogging toward them through the trees. She burst out into the open, waving her arms, just as Mr. Penderwick once more stepped hard on the brakes. The whole family was out of the car in an instant, running to meet her.

"Churchie, Churchie!" Jane and Batty threw themselves at her, while Skye danced impatiently in circles.

"Jeffrey, what's happened to Jeffrey?"

Churchie was too winded for anything but huffing and panting until everyone thought they'd explode with not knowing. Finally she managed, "Thank goodness I caught you. Oh, my beautiful girls, I'm going to miss you so."

"But, Churchie—Jeffrey—" said Skye.

"I know, dear. Just hold on and he'll tell you himself in a jiffy. He cut through the hedge to the cottage in case you hadn't left and sent me this way in case you had—and here he comes. I can hear him shouting."

Now they could hear him, too, yelling STOP and

WAIT and PLEASE, and then they could see him—
what joy!—rounding the curve, his legs moving so fast
they were a blur. Like lightning, the four girls were off
and running toward him, and a moment later Jeffrey
had disappeared under a pile of Penderwicks. When
he came up for air, he was laughing and talking as fast
as he could. "I'm sorry I'm late, but Mother just made
the phone call to the school this morning, and they
said yes and—"

"Hold on!" Skye waved her arms in front of his
face.

"Start again," said Rosalind.

He smiled around at them. "Everything's okay now."

"Jeffrey!" That was Jane, frantic with curiosity.

He paused and now he was teasing them. At last he
said, "I don't ever have to go to Pencey."

The cheering was so loud and long that—as
Churchie swore later—the Arundel birds fled and
didn't come back until the next spring. When the
Penderwicks' throats finally gave out, Jeffrey started
over at the beginning. "After we went back to the
house yesterday, Dexter wanted me to go to my room,
but Mother said she wanted to talk. So we talked
and then she cried, and we talked and she cried and
that went on forever. Then Dexter went home and
Mother and I talked some more, and you were right,
Rosalind. I was finally able to make her understand

258

about Pencey, and that was great, and she even said I never had to go to West Point if I didn't want to. And then we started to talk about Dexter—" Jeffrey's smile faded a little.

"She's still marrying him?" said Skye.

He nodded. "It could be worse, I guess."

"She could be marrying a serial killer."

"Or a werewolf," said Jane.

"Or a—" Batty couldn't think of anything worse than a werewolf.

"Anyway, I told Mother if she's going to marry him, I really would prefer to go to that boarding school in Boston—you know, the one I told you about—and this morning she called them and they'll take me in September as long as it turns out I'm not a complete moron, and Mother promised she'd drive me to Boston herself, just me and her, without Dexter. And wait! I haven't told you the best part!" Jeffrey held up his palm for high fives all around. "She said I'm allowed to take a music class at the conservatory! Just one class for now, but it's a beginning, right?"

"Oh, yes! Oh, yes!" they all shouted, and if any Arundel birds had stayed behind after the last outburst, they surely left now. Jane and Batty couldn't stop hopping up and down, and Skye kept tossing both her and Jeffrey's camouflage hats into the air, and Rosalind went so far as to kiss Jeffrey on the cheek, there having been so much kissing already that day. Then Mr. Penderwick, after getting the good news in a calmer fashion from Churchie, came over and shook Jeffrey's hand and slapped him on the back, and then Churchie started to cry, and then Jane started to cry, and then Batty, and when even Skye started to cry, it really was time to go home. So for the third time, the Penderwicks loaded themselves into the car, but this time with light hearts and consciences and the glad relief that comes with happy endings.

Skye rolled down her window and Jeffrey leaned in. Churchie stood behind him, her hand affectionately on his shoulder.

"We're going to miss you, Jeffrey," said Jane.

"We'll visit him in Boston," said Rosalind.

"And I'll visit you in Cameron," said Jeffrey.

"Just remember, if you don't, I'll kill you," said Skye.

"I'll remember," said Jeffrey. "Good-bye, Hound. Stay out of trouble."

Hound wagged his tail cheerfully. Just thinking about trouble made him happy.

"Okay, everybody, let's go," said Mr. Penderwick. "Good-bye, Jeffrey. Congratulations again and the very best of luck!"

"Good-bye! Good-bye!" said everyone.

And off they went again, down the long driveway. Well, off they went for about twenty yards, anyway. Because by then Batty was pleading with her father to stop the car just one last time, that she had something to do.

"What is it, Batty?" said Rosalind.

"Something very important. Please stop, Daddy. It won't take long."

So Mr. Penderwick stopped and Jane let Batty out her side. Everyone hung out their windows to watch Batty run back toward the cottage, calling to Jeffrey. He walked forward to meet her.

"What's she up to?" said Skye.

"She's telling him something," said Jane.

"He looks surprised," said Rosalind.

"Oh, oh, oh, oh—do you see what she's doing?" said Jane.

"She's—I can't believe this—she's taking off her wings and giving them to Jeffrey!" said Skye.

"He's putting them on!" said Jane.

"My wise little Batty," said Mr. Penderwick. "*Maxima debetur puellae reverentia.*"

With that, there was nothing left to say. They all sat in silence while Batty trotted back, climbed in over Jane, and settled in her seat.

"Now we can go," said Batty.

"But, Batty, your wings," said Rosalind.

"I told Jeffrey he could borrow them."

"What did he say?" said Skye.

"He said thank you."

"Nothing else?"

261

"Yes, he said good-bye for now."

"That's nice," said Jane. "I like that."

"Hound, say good-bye for now," said Batty.

"Woof!" said Hound.

Then they were gone.

The magic continues in

THE PENDERWICKS ON GARDAM STREET

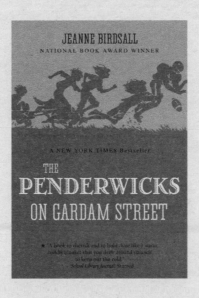

CHAPTER ONE
Rosalind Bakes a Cake

Rosalind was happy. Not the kind of passionate, thrilling happy that can quickly turn into disappointment, but the calm happy that comes when life is steadily going along just the way it should. Three weeks earlier, she'd started seventh grade at the middle school, which was turning out not to be as overwhelming as rumored, mostly because she and her best friend, Anna, shared all the same classes. And it was late September, and the leaves were on the verge of bursting into wild colors—Rosalind adored autumn. And it was a Friday afternoon, and although school was all right, who doesn't like weekends better?

On top of all that, Aunt Claire was coming to visit

for the weekend. Beloved Aunt Claire, whose only flaw was that she lived two hours away from the Penderwicks' home in Cameron, Massachusetts. But she tried to make up for it by visiting often, and now she was arriving this evening. Rosalind had so many things to tell her, mostly about the family's summer vacation, three wonderful weeks at a place called Arundel in the Berkshires. There had been many adventures with a boy named Jeffrey, and for a while Rosalind had thought that she might be in love with another boy—an older one—named Cagney, but that had come to nothing. Now Rosalind was determined to stay away from love and its confusions for many years, but still she wanted to talk it all over with her aunt.

There was lots to get done before Aunt Claire arrived—clean sheets on the bed, clean towels in the bathroom, and Rosalind wanted to bake a cake—but first she had to pick up her little sister Batty at Goldie's Day Care. She did so every day on the walk home from school, and even that was part of her happiness. For this was the first year her father had given her the responsibility for her sisters after school and until he came home. Before now, there had always been a babysitter, one or another of the beautiful Bosna sisters, who lived down the street from the Penderwicks. And though the Bosnas had been good babysitters as well as beautiful, Rosalind considered herself much too old now—twelve years and eight months—for a babysitter.

The walk from Cameron Middle School to Goldie's took ten minutes, and Rosalind was on her last minute now. She could see on the corner ahead of her the gray clapboard house, with its wide porch full of toys. And now she could see—she picked up her pace—a small girl alone on the steps. She had dark curls and was wearing a red sweater, and Rosalind ran the last several yards, scolding as she went.

"Batty, you're supposed to stay inside until I get here," she said. "You know that's the rule."

Batty threw her arms around Rosalind. "It's okay, because Goldie's watching me through the window."

Rosalind looked up, and it was true. Goldie was at the window, waving and smiling. "Even so, I want you to stay inside from now on."

"All right. But—" Batty held up a finger swathed in Band-Aids. "I just was dying to show you this. I cut myself during crafts."

Rosalind caught up the finger and kissed it. "Did it hurt terribly?"

"Yes," said Batty proudly. "I bled all over the clay and the other kids screamed."

"That sounds exciting." Rosalind helped Batty into her little blue backpack. "Now let's go home and get ready for Aunt Claire."

Most days the two sisters would linger on their

walk home from Goldie's—at the sassafras tree, with leaves shaped like mittens, and at the storm drain that flooded just the right amount when it rained, so you could splash through without getting water in your boots. Then there was the spotted dog who barked furiously but only wanted to be petted, and the cracks in the sidewalk that Batty had to jump over, and the brown house with flower gardens all around, and the telephone poles that sometimes had posters about missing cats and dogs. Batty always studied these carefully, wondering why people didn't take better care of their pets.

But today, because of Aunt Claire's visit, they hurried along, stopping only for Batty to move to safety a worm that had unwisely strayed onto the sidewalk, and soon they were turning the corner onto Gardam Street, where they lived. It was a quiet street, with only five houses on each side, and a cul-de-sac at the end. The Penderwick sisters had always lived there, and they knew and loved every inch of it, from one end to the other. Even when Rosalind was in a hurry, like today, she noted with satisfaction the tall maples that marched along the street—one in every front yard—and the rambling houses that were not so young anymore, but still comfortable and well cared for. And there was always someone waving hello. Today it was Mr. Corkhill, mowing his lawn, and Mrs. Geiger, driving by with a car full of groceries—and then Rosalind stopped waving back, for Batty had broken into a run.

"Come on, Rosalind!" cried Batty over her shoulder. "I hear him!"

This, too, was part of their everyday routine. Hound, the Penderwicks' dog, always knew when Batty was almost home, and set up such a clamor he could be heard all up and down Gardam Street. So now both sisters were running, and in a moment Rosalind was unlocking their front door, and Hound was throwing himself at Batty as though she'd been away for centuries instead of just the day.

Rosalind dragged Hound back into the house, with Batty dancing alongside in an ecstasy of reunion. Down the hall they all went, through the living room and into the kitchen—where Rosalind opened the back door and shoved the joyful tangle of child and dog into the backyard. She shut the door behind them and leaned against it to catch her breath. Soon Batty would need her afternoon snack, but for now Rosalind had a moment to herself. She could start on the cake, which she'd decided should be a pineapple upside-down one.

Humming happily, she took the family cookbook from its shelf. It had been a wedding gift to her parents, and was full of her mother's penciled notes. Rosalind knew all the notes by heart, and even had her favorites, like the one next to candied sweet potatoes—

An insult to potatoes everywhere. There was no note next to pineapple upside-down cake. Maybe if it was a great success, Rosalind would add her own. She did that sometimes.

"Melt a quarter cup of butter," she read, then put a skillet on the stove, lit the burner under it, and dropped in a stick of butter. Almost right away the butter started to melt, crackling a little, and filling the kitchen with a delicious bakery-ish smell.

"Add a cup of brown sugar." She measured the sugar and dumped it into the skillet. "Stir butter and sugar mixture until dissolved."

The sugar all melted into the butter, Rosalind took the skillet off the stove, opened a can of pineapple slices, and arranged the slices atop the sugar mixture. She stood back and admired her handiwork. "Looks magnificent, Rosy. What a fabulous cook you are."

She went back to the cookbook, humming again, and then noticed a suspicious lack of noise in the backyard. With a glance out the door, she understood why. Batty and Hound were crouched in the forsythia border, peeping into the next-door neighbors' backyard. And not the neighbors to the right, the Tuttles, who'd lived there forever and wouldn't have cared if Batty and Hound watched through the kitchen window while they ate. No, they were spying on the neighbors to the left, the Aaronsons, who'd just moved in. There had been great hopes for these new neighbors. A large family would have been perfect, for there can never be too many children in a neighborhood. The Aaronsons, however, turned out to be a small family indeed—a mother and a little boy just learning to toddle around, but no father, for he'd died before the boy was born. Both the mother and boy had red hair, which was good, as there were no other redheads on the street, but an interesting hair color only goes so far. Mr. Penderwick already knew Ms. Aaronson slightly. They were both professors at Cameron University—he was a botanist and she an astrophysicist—but the rest of the family had not yet been introduced.

Rosalind didn't think that spying should come before introductions.

"Batty!" she called out the door. "Come here!"

Batty and Hound wriggled out of the forsythia and dragged themselves reluctantly to the house. "We're only playing secret agents."

"Play something else, then. The neighbors might not like to be spied on."

"They weren't in their backyard, so they wouldn't know. Anyway, we were actually looking for the cat."

"I didn't know the Aaronsons had a cat."

"Oh, yes, a large orange cat. He usually sits in the window, and Hound loves him already."

Though Hound thumped his tail in agreement, Rosalind had her doubts that love was what he had in mind. She'd never seen him with a cat, but she knew how he felt about squirrels, as did all the squirrels that tried to make their home on Gardam Street. There was, however, no point in arguing with Batty about Hound's innermost feelings, so she changed the subject.

"How about your afternoon snack?"

Batty was never one to turn down a snack, especially when it was cheese, pretzel sticks, and grape juice, and when, like today, Rosalind let her eat it under the kitchen table, which happened to make an excellent hideout for secret agents.

With Batty settled, Rosalind went back to her cooking. "Sift a cup of flour—" But once more she was interrupted, this time by her other two sisters arriving home from school and storming the kitchen.

"Something smells good." This was Skye, her blond hair crammed messily into a camouflage hat. She stuck her finger into the skillet and scooped out a blob of the sugar mixture.

Rosalind tried to wave her off, but Skye dodged around, laughing and licking her finger.

"Call Daddy," said Rosalind. "You're the last one in."

That was the rule after school. While Rosalind was picking up Batty at Goldie's, Skye and Jane were walking home together from Wildwood Elementary School, where they were in sixth and fifth grades, respectively. Whoever was the last to arrive at the house called Mr. Penderwick at the university to let him know all was well.

"Jane, call Daddy," said Skye.

"I'm too distraught about English class," said Jane.

This was unlike Jane, who loved English class more than anything, even soccer, which she adored. Rosalind turned away from the cookbook and looked hard at the third Penderwick sister. She did look upset. There were even traces of tears.

"What happened?" asked Rosalind.

"Miss Bunda gave her a C on her essay," answered Skye, reaching under the table and swiping some of Batty's cheese.

"My humiliation is complete," said Jane. "I'll never be a real writer."

"I told you Miss Bunda wouldn't like it."

"Let me see the essay," said Rosalind.

Jane pulled several crumpled balls of paper out of her pocket and tossed them onto the kitchen table. "I have no profession now. I'll have to be a vagrant."

Rosalind smoothed out the pieces of paper, found page one, and read, *Famous Women in Massachusetts History, by Jane Letitia Penderwick. Of all the women that come to mind when you think of Massachusetts, one stands out: Sabrina Starr.*" She stopped reading. "You put Sabrina Starr in your essay?"

"Yes, I did," said Jane.

Sabrina Starr was the heroine of five books, all of

them written by Jane. Each was about an amazing rescue. So far, Sabrina had saved a cricket, a baby sparrow, a turtle, a groundhog, and a boy. This last, *Sabrina Starr Rescues a Boy,* had been written during the summer vacation at Arundel. Jane considered it her best.

"But your assignment was to write about a Massachusetts woman who was actually once alive."

"Just what I told her. Ouch!" Skye jumped away from the table, for Batty had just pinched her ankle as revenge for the stolen cheese.

"I explained all that," said Jane. "Look at the last page."

Rosalind found the last page. "*Of course, Sabrina Starr is not a real Massachusetts woman, but I wrote about her because she's more fascinating than old Susan B. Anthony and Clara Barton,*" she read. "Oh, Jane, no wonder Miss Bunda gave you a C."

"I got a C because she has no imagination. Who cares about writing essays, anyway, when you can write stories?"

The phone rang and Skye raced for it. "Hi, Daddy, yes, we're all here and we were just about to call you. . . . We're fine, except Jane's upset because she got a C on her essay. . . . Really?" Skye turned to Jane. "Daddy says remember that Leo Tolstoy flunked out of college and went on to write *War and Peace.*"

"Tell him I'll never even get into college at this rate."

Skye spoke into the phone again. "She said she'll never get into college. . . . What? Tell me again. . . . Okay, got it. Good-bye."

"What did he say?" said Jane.

"That you don't have to worry because you have *tantum amorem scribendi.*" Skye said the last three words slowly and carefully, for they were Latin.

Jane looked hopefully at Rosalind. "Do you know *tantum am*—whatever it is?"

"Sorry, our class hasn't gotten much past *agricola, agricolae,*" answered Rosalind. She had just that year started studying Latin in a desperate attempt to understand her father, who was always tossing out phrases in that ancient language. "So far, I'll only know if Daddy says something about being a farmer."

"Fat chance," said Skye. "Since he's a professor."

"How old do I have to be to read *War and Peace?*" asked Jane. "It would soothe my wounds to find a kindred spirit in Mr. Tolstoy."

"Older than ten, that's for sure," said Skye. Unwilling to be pinched in the ankle again, she headed back for the sugar mixture in the skillet, but this time Rosalind was ready with a body block.

"No more," she said. "I'm making a pineapple upside-down cake for Aunt Claire, and you're ruining it."

"Aunt Claire is visiting!" Jane's face lit up. "In my agony, I'd forgotten. *She* will soothe my wounds."

"And while I'm finishing the cake, you two can get the guest room ready for her."

"Homework . . . ," muttered Skye, drifting toward the door.

"You never do homework on Fridays," Rosalind said briskly. "Go."

Despite Skye's attempt to avoid helping, she was an excellent worker, and the next hour at the Penderwick house went smoothly. The clean sheets and towels were taken care of, the living room was straightened up, and, as a special touch, Batty and Hound were both brushed. Just as Rosalind pulled the finished cake out of the oven, Jane's joyful yell rang through the house.

"Aunt Claire's here!"